D0251765

The enemy was even quicker. He was already up, and his booted foot shot toward Longarm's face in a vicious kick. Longarm twisted aside, letting the brutal blow glance off his shoulder. There was still enough power behind it to stun him and knock him flat on his back.

With an incoherent shout of rage, the Mexican launched himself at Longarm with the knife poised to strike down into the big lawman's body. Before the killing stroke could fall, a six-gun blasted somewhere nearby, a pair of shots triggered quickly. Lead lashed into the man's body and twisted him in midair. He crashed to the ground beside Longarm. The knife went spinning away harmlessly.

Longarm turned his head to look above and behind him. He saw Harriet standing there, a smoking gun held leveled in front of her, in both hands. She said, "Is that all of them?"

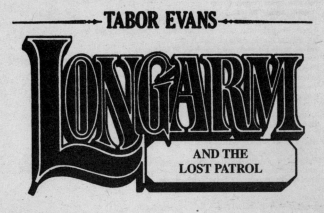

TABOR EVANS

LONGARM

AND THE
LOST PATROL

JOVE BOOKS, NEW YORK

THE BERKLEY PUBLISHING GROUP
Published by the Penguin Group
Penguin Group (USA) Inc.
375 Hudson Street, New York, New York 10014, USA

Penguin Group (Canada), 10 Alcorn Avenue, Toronto, Ontario M4V 3B2, Canada
(a division of Pearson Penguin Canada Inc.)
Penguin Books Ltd., 80 Strand, London WC2R 0RL, England
Penguin Group Ireland, 25 St. Stephen's Green, Dublin 2, Ireland (a division of Penguin Books Ltd.)
Penguin Group (Australia), 250 Camberwell Road, Camberwell, Victoria 3124, Australia
(a division of Pearson Australia Group Pty. Ltd.)
Penguin Books India Pvt. Ltd., 11 Community Centre, Panchsheel Park, New Delhi—110 017, India
Penguin Group (NZ), Cnr. Airborne and Rosedale Roads, Albany, Auckland 1310, New Zealand
(a division of Pearson New Zealand Ltd.)
Penguin Books (South Africa) (Pty.) Ltd., 24 Sturdee Avenue, Rosebank, Johannesburg 2196,
South Africa

Penguin Books Ltd., Registered Offices: 80 Strand, London WC2R 0RL, England

This is a work of fiction. Names, characters, places, and incidents either are the product of the author's imagination or are used fictitiously, and any resemblance to actual persons, living or dead, business establishments, events, or locales is entirely coincidental.

LONGARM AND THE LOST PATROL

A Jove Book / published by arrangement with the author

PRINTING HISTORY
Jove edition / February 2005

Copyright © 2005 by The Berkley Publishing Group

ISBN: 0-515-13888-6

JOVE®
Jove Books are published by The Berkley Publishing Group,
a division of Penguin Group (USA) Inc.,
375 Hudson Street, New York, New York 10014.
JOVE is a registered trademark of Penguin Group (USA) Inc.
The "J" design is a trademark belonging to Penguin Group (USA) Inc.

PRINTED IN THE UNITED STATES OF AMERICA

10 9 8 7 6 5 4 3 2 1

Chapter 1

Longarm had been on army posts all over the West, and he supposed that despite superficial differences, they were pretty much the same all over the world. The tramping of feet as men drilled on the parade ground, the ringing of hammer on anvil from the smithy, the flapping and fluttering of flags . . . those were common sounds no matter where the post was located.

Today he was riding into Fort Stockton, Texas, on a leggy roan horse, leading a chestnut with a dead man tied facedown over the saddle.

The trooper at the guard post gave Longarm and the corpse a wide-eyed stare. "Halt, sir!" he rapped out. "Uh, state your business."

Longarm leaned forward in the McClellan saddle he favored and stood up a little in the stirrups to ease muscles stiff from long hours of riding. He was a tall man, rangy like the horse he rode, with a face weathered to the color of old saddle leather by years of exposure to the elements. He had dark brown hair and sweeping longhorn mustaches of the same shade adorned his upper lip. As he settled back down in the saddle, he thumbed back his flat-crowned, snuff-brown Stetson and then jerked the same thumb at the horse he was leading.

"Got a dead man here," he said dryly. His tone of voice matched the weather, which in West Texas at this time of year—early summer—was already arid.

"I, uh, can see that, sir." The young private struggled with his composure as he asked, "Did you kill him, or find him that way?"

"I'm afraid I killed him," Longarm said gravely. "Seemed like the thing to do at the time, since he was doing his damnedest to shoot holes in my hide. I returned the favor."

"And you brought him here because . . . ?"

"He's one of yours, even though he's out of uniform." Longarm took pity on the youngster and explained. "I'm a federal lawman, son. Deputy U.S. Marshal Custis Long, out of the Denver office." Again he pointed at the dead man with his thumb. "This fella here was a deserter from Fort Bliss, out in El Paso. I got called in when he wasn't satisfied with deserting but decided to rape and murder a couple of women. I tracked him to San Solomon Springs, a ways west of here, and we had it out. He lost. I don't aim to haul him clear back to El Paso. He's already getting a mite ripe. So I thought I'd leave him here and let your commanding officer deal with him."

"Oh," the guard said. "You want to see Colonel Bascomb, then."

Longarm nodded patiently. "I reckon."

He didn't know Bascomb. The last time he'd been in Fort Stockton, Colonel Stilwell had been the post commander. Longarm figured Stilwell had been transferred to another command and this Bascomb fella had replaced him.

The guard turned to point. "The headquarters building is right over there, Marshal."

"I know where it is, son. Been here before. But I'm much obliged anyway."

2

Longarm clucked at the roan and started walking the horse around the parade ground. The guard called after him, "Would you like someone to take charge of the, ah, body, Marshal?"

"That'd be fine," Longarm said over his shoulder. "You know where I'll be."

"Yes, sir!"

Longarm smiled as he heard the kid bawling excitedly for the sergeant of the guard. With the Indians in the area mostly pacified now, except for the occasional band of bronco Apaches that came raiding up from across the Rio Grande, he imagined life at Fort Stockton was pretty peaceful most of the time. That young trooper might not have even seen a dead man in all the time that he'd been wearing the uniform.

Longarm drew more attention as he circled the parade ground. The troops who were drilling stopped to look at him and his grisly cargo before the sergeant in charge of them blasted their ears with profanity and got them moving again.

Several men on the porch of the sutler's store also watched him with great interest as he rode toward them. Longarm didn't pay much attention to them.

He looked again, though, at the woman who stepped out of the building just then. Most men would take a second look at her, no matter where she was. But here on this dusty, sun-splashed army post, she really stood out.

She was in her twenties, with thick, shoulder-length dark red hair and brilliant green eyes. A few freckles were scattered across the bridge of her nose. She was of medium height and curved in all the right places, a fact that her gray dress didn't emphasize but didn't conceal all that much, either.

She met Longarm's gaze with a level expression. He reached up to tug on the brim of his hat and nodded to her as he rode past. She rewarded him with a faint smile.

Longarm didn't know what she was doing there. It was

3

unusual to find a woman on an army post unless she was an officer's wife or daughter.

And he had happened to notice that the pretty redhead wasn't wearing a wedding ring. Maybe the daughter of an officer, then, although she was a little old for that.

It was a question that could wait awhile, until after he had gotten rid of the late Sergeant Amos McKelvey.

Longarm reined to a stop in front of the headquarters building. Like all the other structures in the fort, it was built of logs and adobe, mostly adobe. There was no stockade wall around Fort Stockton. The post was open, a group of frame and adobe buildings clustered around the parade ground.

As Longarm swung down from the saddle, a burly Irish non-com hurried up to him. "Sergeant of the guard, sir," the man said. "Let me take that gentleman over to the hospital for you."

"He ain't no gentleman," said Longarm, "and he's about a day past needing a hospital. But I reckon that's where your morgue is."

"Yes, sir. We'll get him ready for burial." The sergeant wrinkled his nose as he caught a whiff of the corpse. "A quick burial," he added.

"Good idea," Longarm agreed with a nod. He looped the roan's reins around the hitch rack in front of the headquarters building and stepped up onto the porch as the sergeant led the chestnut away.

A corporal was on duty at the adjutant's desk in the outer office. He was already on his feet as Longarm came into the room. "Help you, sir?" he asked.

"I need to see your commanding officer," Longarm said.

"The door's open, and I couldn't help but notice that you've got a dead man with you, sir. I'd suggest that as a civilian, you should contact Sheriff Arquette in the town of Fort Stockton to report . . . whatever it is you've got to report."

4

"Well, that'd be a dandy idea, son, if not for the fact that the fella I brought in is a deserter, as well as a murderer."

"Are you a bounty hunter?"

"Nope. Lawman."

A footstep sounded behind Longarm. He glanced over his shoulder to see a tall, erect major entering the building. The adjutant snapped to attention and saluted.

"At ease, Corporal," the major said. He put his hand out as he approached Longarm. "You'd be Marshal Long?"

"That's right," Longarm said as he shook with the officer.

"Major Jeremiah Ordway," the major introduced himself. His voice had a faint New England twang to it. He was clean-shaven, relatively young, and had an earnest look about him. "I was just over at the hospital when the sergeant of the guard brought the body up. He told me the situation. Colonel Bascomb is in his quarters, but I've sent for him. I'm second-in-command here."

"Pleased to meet you, Major," Longarm said.

Ordway gestured toward a door. "I'm sure it will be all right if we wait for the colonel in his office. Please, after you, Marshal."

The adjutant sprang to open the door for him. Everybody here at the fort was being mighty cooperative, thought Longarm. Sometimes the army didn't worry that much about getting along with civilian lawmen. It looked like these soldier boys were going to make this part of his job easy for a change.

The colonel's office contained a large desk, several chairs, maps of West Texas pinned to the walls, and a photograph of President Rutherford B. Hayes looking suitably presidential. Ordway indicated that Longarm should have a seat in front of the desk. The major leaned a hip on a corner of the desk and asked, "Why don't you tell me what happened, Marshal?"

"Reckon it'd be best if I waited and spun the yarn once, when Colonel Bascomb gets here."

5

"Of course." If Ordway was offended by the answer, he didn't show it. "It shouldn't take very long."

It didn't. Footsteps sounded in the outer office only a couple of minutes later. A thickset officer a little below medium height came into the room after returning the adjutant's salute. He had gray hair and a close-cropped beard. With a curt nod he went around the desk.

"I'm Oliver Bascomb," he said to Longarm in a business-like tone.

"Custis Long," Longarm introduced himself as he shook hands. He liked Bascomb's no-nonsense attitude. "I reckon you heard about the fella I brought in."

"I heard that you claim he's a soldier. You certainly couldn't prove it by his clothes."

"No, he's out of uniform, sure enough. I reckon he couldn't get rid of his army duds quick enough after he deserted from Fort Bliss."

"Do you have any proof of the man's identity?" Bascomb asked.

"Damn fool got rid of his uniform but kept his identification papers, if you'll pardon my French," Longarm said. "He didn't act none too innocent when I caught up to him, neither. He bushwhacked me and tried to kill me."

"What did you do?"

"I didn't let him," Longarm said with a smile.

For a second, Bascomb glared across the desk and Longarm thought he might turn out to be one of those humorless, by-the-book martinets. He had run into that type of officer all too often, all the way back to when he had fought in the Late Unpleasantness as not much more than a gangling farm boy from West-by-God Virginia.

But then Bascomb broke into a grin and said, "Good. I'd hate to think I never got the chance to meet the famous Longarm."

The big lawman grunted. "Heard tell of me, have you?"

"You've lent a hand to the army on several occasions. Word gets around."

Longarm shrugged. "I pack a federal lawman's badge, so I reckon when you come down to it we both work for Uncle Sam. I try to get along and help out when I can."

"I'm pleased to hear that, Marshal. More pleased than you can know." Bascomb sank into his chair. "But for now, why don't you just tell me what happened?"

Longarm obliged this request, briefly explaining how the late Sergeant McKelvey had taken off from Fort Bliss and gone on a spree of violence that had left several people dead.

"Why would he do that?" Major Ordway asked.

"Some hombres just turn into hydrophobia skunks if you give 'em the chance. I don't know what made McKelvey go bad, and I didn't have a chance to ask him 'fore I put a couple o' forty-five slugs through his gizzard. Seemed more important to stop him from ventilating me."

"Yes, of course," Bascomb said. "Go on, Marshal."

"Not much more to tell," Longarm said. "I got on his trail, caught up to him over at San Solomon Springs, and when the smoke cleared he was dead. I put him on his horse and brought him here. Figured it was too far back to El Paso."

Bascomb nodded. "That was wise. We'll take care of the burial and I'll notify the commanding officer over at Bliss that the matter has been brought to a successful conclusion."

"I'd be obliged," Longarm said. He got ready to get to his feet.

"Is there anything else we can do for you?"

He shook his head. "Nope, I don't reckon there is. I thought I'd stay in the town of Fort Stockton for a day or two, until the next train comes through. Sheriff Arquette and I have worked together before, so I figured I'd say howdy to him."

7

"A good man, Sheriff Arquette," Bascomb said with a nod. "Young, but good. I'm sure if you two are friends that he'll be glad to see you."

Longarm started to stand up.

The colonel stopped him by saying quickly, "But if I could have a few more minutes of your time, Marshal . . . ?"

Longarm sank back into the chair. "I don't reckon I'm in much of a hurry, now that I've turned McKelvey over to you folks. What can I do for you, Colonel?"

"I was wondering . . . since you're here, and as you said, we both work for Uncle Sam . . . if I could ask a favor of you."

"I'll be glad to listen to what you've got to say, Colonel," Longarm replied with a shrug.

"You're obviously good at investigating mysteries and tracking people down," Bascomb began.

"Colonel," Major Ordway broke in worriedly, "are you sure you should be discussing this with Marshal Long? After all, it *is* army business."

"Well, the army hasn't done much good at getting to the bottom of it, have they?" Bascomb demanded sharply. "We've sent out search party after search party and none of them have come up with a thing."

"All the more reason to think that one man, and a civilian, at that—"

This time it was the colonel who interrupted. "At ease, Major," he snapped. "I want to see what Marshal Long thinks about this."

"Thinks about what, Colonel?" Longarm asked. "Maybe you'd best get down to brass tacks."

"Indeed," Bascomb said with a crisp nod. "I want you to find something for me, Marshal, if you think it would be all right with your boss for you to lend us a hand."

"What is it you're looking for?"

"A cavalry patrol," Bascomb said.

Longarm's forehead creased in a frown. "A whole patrol?"

"That's right. Fifteen men and the lieutenant who was in command." Bascomb's voice took on a hollow, disbelieving note as he went on, "They rode away from here, Marshal, and they never came back. The whole patrol . . . vanished. Simply vanished."

Chapter 2

Longarm didn't know what to make of that. From the looks of him, Colonel Oliver Bascomb wasn't a crazy man. It made no sense for him to sit there calmly and claim that an entire cavalry patrol had up and disappeared. But that was exactly what he had just done.

Bascomb must have seen the dubious expression on Longarm's face. He said, "I know it's hard to believe. Sixteen soldiers don't just vanish into thin air. But that's what happened. Lieutenant Morgan and his men rode out headed south toward the border on a routine patrol. They never came back. That was over three weeks ago and there's been no sign of them."

"How long were they supposed to be gone?" Longarm asked with a frown.

"Well, as you know, West Texas is a big place. You have to ride a long way to get anywhere. It's not unusual for a patrol to be out for a week and a half, or even two weeks. But when more than two and a half weeks went by without any word, I began to worry."

Longarm nodded slowly and said, "I reckon I can understand that."

"I sent a galloper to Marathon. That's the nearest settlement of any size south of here."

"I've been there," Longarm said. In truth, it would be difficult for the colonel to have named any place west of the Mississippi where Longarm *hadn't* been. He had gotten around a mite during his eventful career.

"No one there has seen the patrol," Bascomb said.

"You mean they never got there?"

"Either that, or they circled around the town for some reason. But I also sent riders to all the ranches in the area." Bascomb shook his head. "Still nothing. No one has seen them."

Longarm tugged at the lobe of his right ear and then raked a thumbnail along his jawline. Those were habitual gestures when he was deep in thought, as he was now.

"Too much time had gone by for you to follow any sort of trail they might have left," he said.

Even though the words weren't really a question, Bascomb nodded and said, "That's right. By the time we realized something was wrong, any tracks the patrol might have left were long gone."

"That's mighty puzzling, all right. Any chance they might have up and deserted?"

"All of them?" Major Ordway exclaimed. "I hardly think that's likely, Marshal. Lieutenant Morgan is a fine young officer, completely devoted to his duty. I can't imagine him deserting."

"Maybe the others didn't leave the decision up to him," Longarm said quietly.

"A mutiny, eh?" Bascomb said. "I suppose it's possible. But Sergeant Vance is a good man, too, a veteran soldier. It wouldn't be like him to turn his back on the oath he swore." The colonel shook his head. "Something has happened to them. You can see why I'm worried, Marshal."

"Yep, I reckon I can. But I don't know where I come into it."

"I want you to find out what happened to that patrol," Bascomb said bluntly. "My men are soldiers, not lawmen. They have no experience at conducting an investigation. You're an old hand at such things, though, Marshal Long."

Longarm couldn't deny that. He had sorted out a heap of messes over the years.

The army was usually pretty touchy about civilians poking into its affairs. This was one time, however, when the army was asking for help and Longarm didn't rightly see how he could turn down the request.

Billy Vail could, though, and until Longarm had wired the chief marshal in Denver and explained the situation to him, he wasn't going to make any promises.

"I'll get in touch with my boss and see if it's all right with him for me to look into this," he offered. "You may have to ask the War Department to send an official request for assistance to the Justice Department, and then Justice can pass it along to me."

"And by that time, who knows what will have happened to my men!" Bascomb exclaimed impatiently. "I don't mean to put you in a bad spot, Marshal, but I need help and I'm not too ashamed to admit it. I'll send a wire to the chief marshal right now if you'd like."

"Why not let me handle that?" Longarm suggested. "It'll probably take until tomorrow to hear back from Denver, but if Marshal Vail doesn't order me directly not to get involved, I reckon I can start scouting around."

Bascomb suddenly looked tired and Longarm realized what a strain the officer was under. "Thank you, Marshal. I suppose that's the best answer I could have hoped for."

"I wouldn't worry too much," Longarm said as he came to his feet. "Those old boys got to be somewhere."

"Yes," Bascomb said, "but are they still alive . . . or dead?"

Longarm couldn't answer that one.

• • •

13

There had been a military post at this spot, off and on, for a little over forty years. Nearby Comanche Springs was an oasis of sorts in this dry country and put out so much water that in recent years farmers had started moving in and irrigating fields for crops. Ranching was still the dominant business in the area, though, and probably always would be, Longarm thought.

The town that had grown up next to the post was also known as Fort Stockton. Already a busy community, the arrival of the railroad a couple of years earlier had really kicked off a growth spurt for the settlement. The telegraph office was located inside the railroad depot, so that was where Longarm headed.

He got a message flimsy and a stub of a pencil from a visor-wearing clerk behind the counter and printed out his message to Billy Vail. He described the situation in as few words as possible so that Henry, the chief marshal's secretary who went over all the deputies' expense accounts, wouldn't kick up too much of a fuss. Then he concluded by asking Vail how he ought to proceed.

Longarm already knew what he was going to do, even though he hadn't admitted as much to Colonel Bascomb. He had an inquisitive mind, and there was no way he could just ride off from a mystery like this without at least poking his nose into it a little. Those missing soldier boys had to have gone somewhere. It would make things a heap simpler in the long run, though, if Vail approved of the investigation.

When he was done, Longarm gave the message to the clerk, paid for it, and said, "I'll be staying at the Pecos House. When the reply comes, you can find me there, or at the Grey Mule Saloon." That was Fort Stockton's leading drinking establishment and one where Longarm could be sure of finding his favorite Maryland rye.

"All right, Marshal," the clerk said. "I'll send a boy to find you as soon as I hear back from Denver."

Longarm nodded and walked back out onto the street,

14

where he had left his horse tied to a hitch rack. He slipped a cheroot from his shirt pocket, put it unlit in his mouth, and untied the reins. He led the roan down the street to a livery stable, made arrangements for the horse's care, and then headed for the hotel to check in, carrying his Winchester and his saddlebags.

The clerk at the Pecos House remembered him from his previous visits and asked, "What brings you to Fort Stockton this time, Marshal?"

"A dead man," Longarm replied. The clerk's eyebrows arched.

Longarm didn't explain further. He just took his key, lugged his saddlebags and Winchester upstairs, and stashed them in his room. Then he left the hotel and walked toward the Grey Mule Saloon. The past couple of weeks had seen him riding some long, hot, dusty trails and he needed to cut that trail dust with a healthy drink of Tom Moore.

The Grey Mule had a stylized drawing of such a critter on the sign that hung above the entrance, reminding Longarm of the famous Bull's Head Saloon in Abilene, Kansas. The explicit sign on the Bull's Head had almost led to shooting between the saloon's owner, gambler Phil Coe, and the town marshal, James Butler "Wild Bill" Hickok. Eventually, Hickok had shot Coe dead, but at least it hadn't been over a bull's pecker.

That would have made for a hell of an epitaph, Longarm thought with a chuckle as he entered the Grey Mule.

At this time of day, late in the afternoon, the place wasn't very busy. Later, when more of the cowboys from the ranches in the surrounding area had had a chance to ride into town, the saloon would do a lot more business. At the moment only half a dozen men stood drinking at the bar and only one of the tables scattered around the room had a poker game going at it.

Longarm walked to the bar, nodded to the balding, mild-appearing drink juggler on the other side of the hardwood, and said, "Maryland rye, Tom Moore if you've got it."

"We've got it," the bartender said in a friendly manner. He turned, took a glass and a bottle from the backbar, and poured the drink.

Longarm tossed back the shot of whiskey and closed his eyes for a second in satisfaction as the liquor lit a warm glow in his belly. As he put the empty glass on the bar, he said, "Let's chase that with a cold beer."

"Coming right up," the bartender replied with a smile. Down the bar, a couple of cowboys joshed each other boisterously.

Longarm heard the batwings flap as someone else came into the saloon. Habit made him glance over his shoulder. One reason he had lasted so long in such a risky profession was that he was a cautious man. He liked to know who was behind him at all times.

He wasn't expecting to see what he saw. The pretty redhead from the fort stood just inside the saloon entrance. A pair of spectacles perched on her nose now, but that didn't make her any less pretty. If anything, Longarm thought, they added a certain appeal, because a fella couldn't help but think about under what circumstances she might take those spectacles *off*.

It was unusual for a respectable woman to come into a place like the Grey Mule, but not unheard of. Still, the bartender arched his eyebrows in surprise as he looked at her. He asked, "Can I help you, ma'am?"

The redhead came toward the bartender and that just naturally brought her toward Longarm, too, since he was standing at the bar right in front of the drink juggler. He gave her a polite nod, just as he had when he rode past her at the fort. She glanced at him but didn't smile. He tried not to be too disappointed.

"I hate to bother you," she said to the bartender. "Have you seen an old man in here recently?"

"An old man?" The bartender shook his head. "No, I don't believe I have. Not this afternoon, anyway. There are some rummies who show up every night . . ."

"No, this would have been within the past hour." The young woman's forehead creased in a worried frown. "I've been trying to keep an eye on him, but he wandered off. Since he has a, ah, fondness for spirits, I thought he might have come in here . . ."

"A relative of yours, ma'am?" the bartender asked gently.

"My uncle," she replied. "Great-uncle, actually, but I always call him Uncle Dan."

"What does he look like? If I see him, I can tell him that you're looking for him."

"He's rather short, only about as tall as me. He has white hair and a beard. He works as a teamster, so he'll be rather roughly dressed. If you do see him, will you tell him that his niece Harriet wants him to come back to the fort?"

"Of course, ma'am," the bartender assured her.

She sighed, her expression a mixture of exasperation and concern. "I suppose I'll have to go all over town looking for him," she said worriedly.

Longarm downed the last of the beer in his mug and said, "Pardon my butting in, ma'am, but it'll be dark soon and a lady like you shouldn't be wandering around town by yourself. It ain't hardly safe."

Those green eyes regarded him coolly. "I appreciate your concern, sir," she said, "but I assure you I'm capable of looking out for myself."

"I don't have a thing in the world to do right now," he said, thinking that he wouldn't be leaving Fort Stockton until he'd heard from Billy Vail and that probably wouldn't be until the next day. "I'd be happy to help you look for your uncle and after we find him, maybe we could have some supper."

17

"And you'd protect me from the ruffians who populate this settlement, is that it?"

"Something like that," Longarm said with a smile.

"And exactly how is it I'm supposed to know that *you're* not one of those very ruffians?" she asked crisply. The touch of feistiness in her voice made Longarm like her that much more. She had the Irish to match her hair.

He grinned. "Well, ma'am, if you don't want to take my word for it, I reckon the commander at the fort and the local sheriff will both vouch for me—"

He didn't get to finish his sentence, because at that moment one of the cowboys from down the bar pushed roughly past him.

"Why don't you let somebody else talk to the gal, mister?" the puncher said, then ignored Longarm as he turned a leering grin on the redhead. "Howdy, ma'am. How about you forget this tall drink o' water and go upstairs with a real man?"

The redhead stiffened and said icily, "What?"

The cowboy, who was just drunk enough to get himself into trouble, poked a thumb at the narrow staircase that led up to the saloon's second floor. "I want to go upstairs with you, honey. We'll have us a nice lil' tumble. I'll treat you right. An' don't worry . . . I got plenty o' money."

The bartender leaned forward and put a hand on the cowboy's arm. "Rance, you'd better back off," he advised. "You're making a mistake here—"

Rance swatted the bartender's hand away. "Don't touch me!" he snapped. He grinned at the redhead again. "Only one I want touchin' me is this little filly here." He swayed toward her. "Gal, you really are pretty, 'specially for a whore."

Her nostrils flared as she drew in a deep breath. Then her hand flashed up and cracked across the cowboy's face. She slapped him hard enough that his head jerked to the side and he stumbled back a step.

But then he caught himself, yelled, "You bitch!" and drew his hand back to return the slap.

His hand had just started forward when Longarm's fingers closed around his wrist like bars of iron.

Chapter 3

The cowboy yelped in pain as Longarm bent his arm behind his back. At the same time, Longarm reached around and plucked the cowboy's gun from its holster. He twisted toward the bar and the young puncher had no choice but to go with him or else have his elbow or shoulder dislocated.

Longarm slammed the cowboy against the bar. The edge of the hardwood drove into the youngster's belly and knocked the wind out of him. He doubled over, huffing and blowing and gasping. Longarm let go of his wrist, planted a boot on the cowboy's backside, and shoved, sending the young man sprawling and sliding facedown in the sawdust that littered the saloon floor.

Longarm opened the loading gate on the cowboy's Colt, tilted the barrel up, and slowly revolved the cylinder so that the bullets in the chambers fell out one by one and plinked to the floor. The gun held five rounds, since its owner obviously was in the habit of carrying the hammer on an empty. When all the chambers were empty, Longarm flipped the loading gate shut and placed the Colt on the bar.

"Did you have to do that?" the redhead demanded angrily.

"He was about to slap you," Longarm said.

"I know that. I slapped him first. Not that that excuses

21

such abominable behavior on his part. But I assure you, I would have dealt with him. What business was it of yours, anyway?"

"I don't hold with being rough on women," Longarm said.

"How chivalrous."

Longarm glanced at the other cowboys along the bar. None of them stepped forward to take up the cause of their friend. In fact, one of them said, "If you're worried about us jumpin' in to back Rance's play, mister, there ain't no need. He's mighty dumb when he gets drunk."

Still breathing hard from having the wind knocked out of him, Rance pushed himself up onto hands and knees and shook his head. He turned to glare at Longarm.

"You son of a bitch!" he said as he started to his feet. "I'll kill you for that!"

Longarm put up a hand, palm out. "Better hold on, son. You're biting off more'n you can swallow. It's best to eat the apple one bite at a time."

"I'll shove an apple down your damn throat!" Rance shouted as he lunged at Longarm, fists swinging.

Before Longarm could do more than set his feet and get ready to defend himself, the redhead plucked up the mug of beer that the bartender had drawn for Longarm and left sitting untouched on the bar. Turning smoothly, she crashed it down on Rance's head. The mug shattered, spraying beer all over the young cowboy.

He stopped short with a confused expression on his face. Then his eyes rolled up in their sockets and his knees folded. He crumpled to the floor, out cold.

The other cowboys looked a little worried now. "Lord, you didn't kill him, did you, ma'am?" one of them asked.

Longarm toed Rance's side and rolled him over onto his back. "He's breathing," the big lawman said. "If you boys are his pards, maybe you best haul him out of here and let him sleep it off somewhere."

"We'll tie him in the saddle and take him back to the ranch." The punchers bent to grab the unconscious man's arms and legs.

Before they could carry him out of the saloon, the batwings parted and a man stepped in carrying a shotgun. He was fairly young, in his mid-twenties, with brown hair and a mustache that he probably should have shaved off since it was never going to come in very good. A tin star was pinned to his vest.

"Somebody passing by saw a ruckus through the window and came to fetch me," the local lawman announced. "What's going on here? Rance isn't dead, is he?"

"Nope, just out cold," Longarm said.

The sheriff looked at him, and the young star packer's eyes widened in recognition. "Marshal Long!" he exclaimed. "It's good to see you again." He walked toward the bar, holding the greener loosely at his side now.

"Good to see you, too, Dewey," Longarm greeted the sheriff as he shook hands.

"It looks like you were telling the truth about the sheriff vouching for you," the redhead commented.

Sheriff Dewey Arquette nodded. "Yes, ma'am, I surely will. This is Deputy U.S. Marshal Custis Long. We've worked together before."

"Told you I was harmless," Longarm said to the redhead with a grin.

"Harmless?" Dewey repeated. He snorted and gestured at the unconscious Rance. "Don't look too harmless to me."

"I didn't do that," Longarm said mildly.

"Who did?"

Longarm nodded to the redhead. "The lady here."

Dewey stared at her. "Miss Summers? You walloped that cowboy?"

"I was simply trying to prevent more trouble," she said.

"I reckon you put a stop to it, all right," Dewey said with a shrug. "Was he annoyin' you?"

"He was very insulting."

"That's true, Sheriff," one of Rance's friends said. "Rance was bein' a jackass, as per usual. You want we should take him over to the jail, so's you can lock him up?"

Dewey shook his head. "No, as long as no damage was done . . ." He glanced at the bartender.

"Just one busted mug, Sheriff," the man replied. "Only other things that got hurt were Rance's head and his pride."

"Well, then, I won't charge him with disturbing the peace." Dewey dug a coin out of the unconscious puncher's pocket and handed it to the bartender. "That'll cover the mug. You fellas get him out of here and tell him I said not to come back to town until he learns how to behave himself."

The cowboys agreed and hauled Rance out of the saloon.

"I'd still like to know exactly what went on here," Dewey continued.

"It was nothing important," the redhead said. She had referred to herself as Harriet, Longarm recalled, and Dewey, who evidently knew her, had called her Miss Summers.

Harriet Summers . . . it was a nice name, and it suited her.

"I suppose I shouldn't have come in here in the first place," she went on, "but I was looking for my uncle Dan. You haven't seen him, have you, Sheriff?"

"Not lately," Dewey replied. "I'm sure he's around, though. He can't get into too much trouble here in Fort Stockton."

Harriet rolled her eyes. "You don't know my uncle." She turned back to Longarm. "If your offer still holds to help me look for him . . ."

He tried not to grin too much. "Oh, I reckon you trust me now, since I defended your honor?"

"I trust you since I now know that you're a lawman and a friend of Sheriff Arquette's as well." The worried tone came back into her voice. "And I do want to find my uncle before something happens to him."

"I'll take a look around town, ma'am," Dewey offered. "With you and Marshal Long searching, too, I'm sure we'll turn up your uncle in no time."

Before leaving the saloon, Longarm dropped a coin on the bar. "For the rye and the beer," he said.

"You never got to drink the beer," the bartender pointed out.

"No, but the show was worth it," Longarm said. He followed Dewey and Harriet out of the saloon.

When they were outside, Dewey said, "I'll start down at the other end of the street and we can work toward each other. You reckon he's in one of the saloons, ma'am?"

"I would wager on that," she said. "If I were the wagering sort."

"Don't like to gamble, eh?" Longarm said as he and Harriet started across the street toward another saloon. Dewey walked quickly toward the other end of the settlement with the shotgun now tucked under his arm.

"Gambling is just throwing money away," she said. "I work with figures all day long. I know how numbers add up . . . and how they don't."

"Bookkeeper, are you?"

"That's right. I work at the sutler's store, at the fort."

"Sort of unusual for a woman to have that job, ain't it?"

"I'm sorry to say that most women don't have the necessary education to do such a job. I'm not most women, though."

Longarm nodded and said dryly, "I'm starting to get that idea."

They hadn't even reached the saloon that was their destination when an old man pushed out through the batwings. "Uncle Dan!" Harriet exclaimed.

The old-timer wore a pair of overalls and a battered hat with the brim pushed up. He wiped the back of a gnarled hand across his mouth and flinched a little as Harriet hurried toward him.

25

"Now, gal, don't go to fussin' at me," he said. "I just needed to wet my whistle a mite. I didn't get all likkered up, if that's what you're worried about."

"You know you shouldn't be drinking at all," she scolded him. "It's bad for your stomach, not to mention the fact that you usually get in some sort of argument every time you go in a saloon!"

"Well, I didn't this time," he pointed out. He glanced at Longarm and nodded. "Howdy, mister. You a friend o' my great-niece?"

"I hope to be," Longarm said. "We ran into each other a little while ago and since she was looking for you, I offered to help."

"Well, I'm obliged, but you can see for yourself there wasn't no need to be worried. I'm fine as frog hair." The old-timer stuck out a paw. "Dan Boldin."

"Custis Long," Longarm introduced himself as he shook hands. "Pleased to meet you, Mr. Boldin."

"Aw, hell, call me Uncle Dan. Ever'body does."

"All right," Longarm said with a grin.

Harriet turned to him. "Marshal, would you go tell Sheriff Arquette that he can stop searching for Uncle Dan?"

"Marshal!" the old-timer exclaimed before Longarm could say anything. "You're a lawman, son?"

Longarm nodded. "Deputy U.S. marshal out of Denver."

Uncle Dan looked at Harriet. "You sicced the law on me?"

"Marshal Long was just helping me as a friend," she explained. "He wasn't acting in any official capacity."

Uncle Dan blew out a gusty breath. "I'm glad to know that. I don't need no federal lawdog after me."

Longarm grinned and said, "Nope, no federal charges against you, old-timer, leastways none that I know of."

Uncle Dan frowned. "Old-timer, is it? I'll have you know I can handle a team better'n any young rapscallion!

26

Work harder and go longer'n any of 'em, too! Why, in my day—"

"That's enough, Uncle Dan," Harriet said, laying a hand on his arm. "Let's go back to the fort." She looked at Longarm. "Thank you again, Marshal."

"You know," Longarm said before she could walk away, "I'd surely admire to have dinner with you this evening, ma'am. That is, if you don't have any other plans."

"What other plans would she have?" Uncle Dan asked with a cackling laugh. "Only been here a month and she's done scared off all the other young fellas around here!"

"You hush!" she said sharply. "I've done no such thing." She looked at Longarm again. "I appreciate the offer, Marshal, but—"

"I'm probably just going to be in Fort Stockton for one night," he said. "I reckon I can find some hash house and eat by myself . . ."

"You don't want to make him do that, gal," Uncle Dan put in, his blustery irritation of a few moments earlier seemingly forgotten. "He must be an upstandin' fella, or he wouldn't be a marshal."

"I suppose you're right," Harriet finally agreed with a sigh. She nodded at Longarm. "All right, Marshal, I'll have dinner with you. Just don't get any ideas."

"Not a single solitary one, ma'am," Longarm lied. It was impossible for a normal man to be around such a beautiful woman for very long and not have a few notions sneak into his head.

"Do you know Delgado's Restaurant?"

"No, ma'am, but I reckon I can find it. Fort Stockton ain't all that big a place."

"All right, then. I'll see you there at six-thirty."

Longarm nodded. That would give him time to get cleaned up a little before he met her for dinner. He would find the sheriff, too, and pass along the news that Uncle Dan was safe.

He found Dewey Arquette coming out of a hole-in-the-wall bar down at the other end of the street, close to the livery where Longarm had left the horses. "You can call off the hunt," he said. "Miss Summers and I found her uncle."

"I'm glad to hear it," Dewey said as he thumbed back his hat. "I could tell she was worried. No real need for it, as far as I can see, but still . . ."

"The old man's not a troublemaker?"

"She keeps too tight a rein on him for him to get into any trouble. He drives a supply wagon for the army and when he's not working, Miss Harriet watches him like an old mother hen. Those two are never far apart."

Longarm nodded. "I wonder if he's planning on coming along when I have supper with her tonight."

"Supper?" Dewey let out a low whistle. "You haven't changed, Marshal. Still got quite an eye for the ladies. And Miss Harriet is a sure-enough eyeful, no disrespect intended."

"You sound a mite smitten yourself, old son," Longarm said with a grin.

Dewey shook his head. "Nope. I'm courtin' one of the teachers at the school. We've got two now, you know."

"Two schools?"

"No, two teachers. One of 'em is sort of old and dried up, but the other one . . . well, she's really sweet."

Longarm let out a laugh. "Dewey, if I didn't know better, I'd say you was blushing."

"Just never you mind about that." The young lawman suddenly grew solemn. "But say, Marshal, if you've got a few minutes, I'd sure like it if you'd come down to the office and have a cup of coffee with me. There's something I'd like to talk to you about."

"Law business?" asked Longarm, sensing that something was troubling Dewey.

"More like outlaw business," the star packer said grimly.

Chapter 4

"It's been a couple of years since you've been in these parts," Dewey said once they were seated in the sheriff's office. He sat behind the scarred, paper-littered desk while Longarm half-sprawled on an old couch with a busted spring or two. They had cups of coffee poured from the battered pot on the black cast-iron stove in the corner.

"That's right," Longarm agreed. "I haven't kept up real good with what's been going on around here. But from what I've heard, you've been doing a good job since you took over as sheriff."

"Good enough to get elected on my own last year." Dewey had been promoted from deputy when the previous sheriff had met an untimely end and had served out that term. He sighed as he went on, "That may not be the case next election, though."

"What's wrong?"

"For the past year or so, a gang of owlhoots has been raising holy hell all over West Texas, from the Big Bend up to the High Plains. Mostly, though, they've been operating within a couple of hundred miles of here, which makes some folks think that their hide-out is somewhere in these parts."

"You've tried to track them down?" Longarm asked.

Dewey nodded. "I sure have, on my own and with several posses. No luck so far. I even asked the army for some help. Colonel Bascomb sent out patrols to look for the gang and they didn't do any better than I did."

Longarm frowned. Bascomb hadn't mentioned anything about a gang of outlaws terrorizing the region. He had said that the missing troopers had been out on a routine patrol. But maybe that included looking for owlhoots, these days.

"How big a gang are we talking about?"

"Close to twenty men, from the reports I've read," Dewey replied. "They've hit banks in several towns, stopped trains and robbed the express cars and the passengers half a dozen times, even held up a stagecoach or two. Not long ago I heard that somebody had hit a mule train bringing a shipment of gold up from the mines below the border and wiped out every single one of the men with it. I'm convinced the same bunch was responsible for that."

"Could be," Longarm mused. "I've run across gangs like that before. Snake-blooded killers, most of them."

"That's right," Dewey said. "And even though they haven't struck here in Fort Stockton, they've been close enough so that people think I ought to be able to catch them." He hesitated. "I could use some help, Marshal."

Longarm sipped his coffee and didn't say anything. He mulled the request over in his mind.

He had ridden into Fort Stockton intending to turn over the corpse of the late and unlamented Sergeant McKelvey and then rest up a mite before heading back to Denver, where he was sure Billy Vail would have another job waiting for him. But instead of things going as planned, he'd had two pleas for help, the first from Colonel Bascomb and now this one from Sheriff Dewey Arquette.

It could be, he thought, that the two were related. If that missing cavalry patrol had run into the outlaws, there was a good chance that the troopers were dead. Otherwise they would have returned to the fort by now. Longarm could easily imagine the soldiers riding into an ambush and being cut down by volleys of owlhoot lead . . .

Until he knew more, though, he wasn't going to speculate. Instead, he said, "There's a chance I'll be around here for a spell, Dewey. I reckon I could keep my eyes open and an ear to the ground."

"I'll really appreciate anything you come up with, Marshal. I need a break in this case."

Longarm drained the rest of the coffee from the cup and got to his feet. "I'll head on over to the Pecos House and then Miss Summers and I are supposed to meet for dinner at Delgado's Restaurant, in case you need to find me."

Dewey summoned up a smile and said, "Don't worry, I won't disturb you unless it's a real emergency. Enjoy your evening, Marshal."

"I intend to," Longarm said as he went out.

The Pecos House provided bathtubs and hot water to its guests—for an extra price, of course—and Longarm availed himself of that service. By the time he came back downstairs he had bathed, shaved, and dressed himself in clean clothes.

He smelled of bay rum and instead of the range clothes he had been wearing earlier, now he sported a brown tweed suit, a white shirt, and a black string tie. A silver chain looped across the front of his vest. At one end of the chain was a big silver pocket watch; at the other, like a deadly fob, was a two-shot, .41 caliber derringer that had saved his life on numerous occasions.

He asked the gent at the desk for directions to Delgado's. When he got there, the restaurant proved to be a pretty fancy place, at least for West Texas. Several cut-glass chandeliers provided the lighting and instead of checkered cloths, the tables were covered with fine Irish linen.

Harriet Summers was already there, sitting at one of the tables. She smiled and lifted a hand in greeting as Longarm took off his hat and approached.

"Good evening, Marshal," she said as he sat down. "You look somewhat different."

"Better, I hope," Longarm said with a grin. "Washing off two weeks of trail dust usually improves a fella's appearance."

"Yes, indeed."

"I ain't a patch on you, though," he went on. "I reckon you're just about the prettiest woman this side of New Orleans."

"Please, Marshal. I'm not accustomed to flattery."

"You should be," he told her bluntly. "And it's not flattery, just the truth."

She wore a dark green gown that went well with her red hair and fair skin. Her hair had been washed and brushed until it looked even thicker and softer than it had earlier. She still wore her spectacles. They glittered in the light from the chandelier. Longarm studied her green eyes intently through them.

She blushed under his scrutiny. "Really, Marshal, you're too bold," she said. "You're embarrassing me."

"I'm sorry. I sure didn't mean to."

A waitress in a black dress and white apron came over, dispelling the slight sense of awkwardness that had come over them. Longarm ordered steak with all the trimmings for both of them.

"Where's your uncle this evening?" he asked when the waitress was gone. "I thought he might be having dinner with us."

"No, I left him at the fort with some of his cronies. They'll keep an eye on him and make sure he doesn't get into trouble."

Remembering what Dewey had said about the way Harriet rode herd on her great-uncle, Longarm said, "You know, I reckon a fella like Uncle Dan has been to see the elephant a time or two. He can probably take care of himself just fine."

"He'd like to think so, anyway. But I know my uncle, Marshal, and I know what's best for him."

Longarm shrugged, unwilling to push the matter and provoke an argument. He didn't want to spoil this dinner and whatever might come after it, although he certainly wasn't counting on a damned thing where that was concerned. Uncle Dan was old enough to deal with his greatniece if he didn't like the way she treated him.

"Why don't you call me Custis?" he suggested. "I remember your uncle saying that you'd only been here in Fort Stockton for a month?"

"That's right. We came here from Dallas. I wanted to see more of the West and Uncle Dan was glad to get back to the sort of life that he enjoys."

"What do you think so far?"

Harriet smiled. "I like it. Fort Stockton is a welcome change from Dallas. The settlement has its rough edges, of course, but most of the people are friendly and it's a growing community. I enjoy my work at the fort, too. Colonel Bascomb and Major Ordway are fine gentlemen as well as good officers. I live a very satisfying life." She paused and then added somewhat wistfully, "If a bit of a lonely one at times."

Longarm thought of Uncle Dan's comment about Harriet scaring off all the young men in the area, but he didn't mention it. That old saying about discretion being the better part of valor had a lot of truth to it, in his opinion, especially where womenfolks were concerned.

"Well, I hope you're not lonely this evening," he said.

She smiled. "No, for a change, I'm not. Thank you for talking me into this, Custis." Her hand stole across the table and her fingers touched his for a second. "Now, tell me about your work as a United States marshal."

"Oh, there ain't much to tell. It's pretty boring. A lot of paperwork, mostly."

"It wasn't paperwork that brought in that deserter whose body you left at the post this afternoon."

"Well, no, there was a little shooting involved there," Longarm admitted.

"Do people shoot at you very often?"

"More than I'd like," Longarm said truthfully.

For the next few minutes they chatted about Longarm's job. He downplayed the dangers of it as much as he could. When the waitress brought their steaks they dug in and Longarm was glad to see that Harriet ate with a hearty appetite. He never had cottoned much to gals who just picked at their food like they were afraid of it.

When they were done the waitress brought a pot of coffee. Longarm asked her about adding a dollop of brandy in their cups, but the woman just looked at him severely and said, "Sir, this is a restaurant, not a barroom."

"Sorry," Longarm muttered. When the waitress was gone and he looked across the table at Harriet, he saw a twinkle of amusement in her eyes.

"She put you in your place."

"I reckon." He shrugged. "But I'll live."

Harriet lowered her voice. "If you'd like a drink, I won't object. I don't expect a man to be a teetotaler."

"Maybe I'll drop in at the Grey Mule later."

"I'm surprised you don't have a bottle in your room."

Longarm's eyes narrowed. "I could get one," he said.

"I take a small dram myself, from time to time. For medicinal purposes, of course. An occasional bit of whiskey keeps the digestive system cleaned out."

Longarm didn't say anything for a moment. Then he commented, "No offense, ma'am—"

"Call me Harriet, please."

"No offense, Harriet, but you're a mite different than most women."

34

"Thank you. Now, are you going to ask me up to your hotel room or not? Or do you think I'm being much too forward?"

"You're more than welcome to come up. I'll even get that bottle we were talking about."

"Good. We'll have to be discreet, though. You leave first, and then I'll come up the back stairs at the hotel in ten minutes or so."

Well, at least she didn't believe in being coy about it, thought Longarm. He nodded. "That'll give me time to stop and pick up that bottle."

She lifted her coffee cup and smiled wordlessly over it. Her green eyes, shining through the lenses of the spectacles, were full of promise.

Longarm got to his feet, picked up his hat, and nodded to her. "It was a pleasant evening, Miss Summers. Thank you for the honor of your company."

"You're very welcome, Marshal Long," she replied, keeping up the pretense that they were parting for the night.

Longarm left the restaurant, paying for their meals on his way out. He paused on the boardwalk just outside the door and took a cheroot from his vest pocket. He fished out a lucifer, snapped it into life on an iron-hard thumbnail, and set fire to the gasper. Then, trying not to look too jaunty about it, he headed down the street to the Grey Mule to buy a bottle of Tom Moore.

When he got back to the Pecos House, he picked up his key at the desk and asked, "Anybody looking for me?" He thought a reply might have come from Billy Vail, although he didn't really expect to hear from the chief marshal until the next day.

"No, not a soul, Marshal," the clerk replied. He eyed the bottle in Longarm's hand. "Are you expecting company?"

"Nope, just replenishing my provisions," Longarm said, chuckling. He rolled the cheroot from one corner of his mouth to the other and turned toward the stairs.

As he climbed to the second floor, he thought about Harriet Summers. So far, she had proven to be full of surprises and the unexpected was always intriguing in a woman.

Of course, it was possible she might get cold feet and not show up after all. In that case, Longarm would be disappointed but not overly surprised. It was one thing to flirt in a crowded, well-lit restaurant. Slipping into a hotel through the back entrance and visiting a man's room at night was another matter entirely.

He went down the second-floor corridor to his room, walking quietly out of habit. Another habit made him glance down before he put the key into the lock. When he'd left the room earlier, he had placed a matchstick between the door and the jamb, just a few inches off the floor. The stick was so short it was barely visible.

But it *was* visible and hadn't been disturbed. No one had been in his room, at least not through this door, and since there was no balcony outside the single window, he figured it was unlikely he'd had any visitors. He put the key in the lock and turned it.

He was about to go in when the door at the rear of the hallway opened. Longarm paused and turned toward it, thinking that Harriet had gotten there a little sooner than he expected her.

But it wasn't Harriet who stepped through the door. It was two men with their hat brims pulled down and bandannas pulled up over the lower halves of their faces, hiding their identities.

That right there would have been enough to tell Longarm that something was wrong, even without the guns in their hands that suddenly blasted smoke and lead at him.

Chapter 5

Longarm's instincts and reflexes, honed to a fine edge by years of finding himself in dangerous situations, took over instantly. His left hand held the neck of the whiskey bottle. A flick of his wrist sent it spinning toward the two masked gunmen. At the same time his right hand flashed across his body, darting under his coat to close around the butt of the Colt .45 in its cross-draw rig, and his right foot kicked the door, knocking it open.

He went through the door in a rolling dive, even as bullets scorched through the air where he had been only an eyeblink earlier.

As the thunder of the gunshots still echoed in the hallway, a rush of footsteps told Longarm the bushwhackers weren't going to give up. He rolled over, came up in a crouch, and threw himself behind the bed as the men fired around the corner of the open door. Slugs smacked into the mattress. It stopped some of the bullets, but a couple went all the way through and blasted splinters from the floor only inches from Longarm's head.

As the gunmen ducked back, he popped up and fired a pair of shots through the wall next to the door. The bullets punched through the thin boards. He was rewarded by a yelp of pain.

A second later one of the bushwhackers staggered into the doorway, reeling from a wound in his chest. Blood welled between the fingers of the hand he held pressed to the bullet hole. "You've killed me, you bastard!" he croaked as he charged Longarm. "But I'll take you with me . . . to hell . . . !"

The big lawman fired over the bed again. This bullet caught the gunman in the throat and threw him backward. Blood spurted from the torn artery and sprayed across the comforter on the bed and the thin rug on the floor. The man landed in a gory heap in the doorway. His gun slipped from nerveless fingers.

Longarm leaped up. He heard running footsteps again, but this time they were going away. The other bushwhacker was trying to escape. Now that the odds were even, he had lost his appetite for the fracas.

Longarm bounded over the bloody corpse and slipped a little as his foot came down in a puddle of spreading crimson. That slip saved his life. A bullet sizzled by his ear, so close he could feel the wind-rip of its passage.

He caught his balance and snapped a shot at the second gunman, who had paused at the rear door of the hotel to throw lead at him again. Longarm's slug struck the man in the left arm and knocked him out onto the landing at the top of the rear stairs.

The man still had his gun in his right hand. As he caught his balance, his face contorted from the pain of his wounded arm and he lifted the revolver again, determined to carry out his bloody mission.

Longarm had no choice. He shot the bushwhacker again and this time the bullet drove into the man's chest, throwing him back against the railing. He flipped up and over it and plunged to the ground in the alley that ran behind the hotel. Longarm heard the thud as he landed.

Longarm's Colt was empty. He reached into his pocket for fresh shells and thumbed them into the cylinder before he walked down the hall to the back door. By that time there was a lot of yelling downstairs. Someone shouted, "Send for the sheriff!"

Dewey would have his hands full when he got here, Longarm thought grimly.

He was worried about Harriet. She had been planning to climb those rear stairs right about now. What if she had come along just as the two bushwhackers did? Would they have harmed her if she'd caught them about to sneak into the hotel?

Or had she been back there at all? he suddenly asked himself. His mouth drew into a tight line under the sweeping longhorn mustaches. Was it coincidence that she had sent him back to his hotel room just in time for two gunmen to ambush him? She had even known that he was going to stop at the saloon to pick up a bottle of Maryland rye. That slight delay would have given her time to leave the restaurant and send the two bushwhackers after him.

That was crazy, Longarm told himself with a slight shake of his head. Maybe he had been a lawman for too long. He had absolutely no reason to suspect that Harriet Summers might be mixed up in this attempt on his life.

But, he told himself, he had no reason to think she wasn't, either, other than the fact that she had red hair and was mighty pretty and had just had a nice dinner with him. When you came right down to it, all that didn't mean a damned thing.

Holding the Colt ready to fire, he stepped out onto the landing and swept the barrel down to cover the alley. It was dark back there behind the hotel, but a little light came from the street and from windows in the building. He saw a shape sprawled motionless in the shadows and knew it was the fallen gunman.

Longarm clattered down the steps and struck a match

when he reached the bottom. The glare from the flame glittered on the glassy, lifeless eyes of the dead man. Longarm muttered a curse. With both of the bushwhackers dead, that didn't leave anybody to explain why they had wanted to kill him.

After holstering the Colt, Longarm knelt next to the corpse and used his free hand to search through the man's pockets. He didn't find anything except fifty dollars in gold pieces and the makin's. He pulled down the bandanna and saw a rough-featured, beard-stubbled face. As far as Longarm could remember, he had never seen the man before in his life.

"Hey! Who's down there?"

The shouted question came from the landing at the top of the stairs. Longarm recognized the voice of the young sheriff.

"It's me, Dewey," he called up as he dropped the lucifer just before it burned down to his fingers. "Marshal Long."

Dewey clumped down the stairs carrying a Winchester. He said, "When I heard that somebody was shooting up the Pecos House, I figured you must be mixed up in it, Marshal. I reckon the dead man upstairs is some of your work?"

"Yeah, him and his pard tried to ventilate me as I was going into my room. They came up the stairs and through the back door."

"Were they trying to rob you?"

Longarm shook his head. "I don't think so. They didn't say anything, just came in with masks over their faces and started blazing away at me. This one's got fifty bucks in his pocket, and I reckon if you check the other one, he'll have about the same amount of dinero on him."

"Hired gunmen," Dewey said heavily. "Somebody paid them to kill you."

"That's what it looks like to me," Longarm agreed.

"Who'd want to do that? You just rode into town a few hours ago."

Longarm ran his thumbnail along his jaw as he frowned. "I don't rightly know. I've made a lot of enemies over the years in this job, though. I reckon somebody who's got a grudge against me could have spotted me and hired these old boys to let some daylight through me."

"We may never know for sure," Dewey said with a sigh.

"Nope, we may not," Longarm agreed.

He didn't intend to let it go that easily, though. For one thing, he wanted to have another talk with Harriet Summers. But he realized that he didn't know where she lived. He might have to wait until morning and see her at the army post.

Dewey canted the Winchester over his shoulder. "I'd better go back inside and try to calm everybody down. The way they're carrying on, you'd think Santa Anna was coming down the street with the whole blasted Mexican army."

"There was a lot of lead flying around for a minute or two. I don't blame folks for being a mite spooked."

"I'll send somebody to fetch the undertaker, too. He'll have plenty of work. I expect you'll want to change rooms? That is, if you even want to stay here tonight."

"I don't mind staying," Longarm said. "I'll want a room without so much blood on the floor and the bed, though."

Dewey hurried off alongside the hotel, heading for the main street. Longarm climbed the stairs, back to the second floor. He found quite a few people, a mixture of hotel guests and townspeople, standing in the hall, staying well back from the corpse still sprawled in the doorway of Longarm's room.

"Nothing to worry about, folks," he told them as he walked past. "The shooting's all over."

For now anyway, he thought, but he kept that to himself. It seemed likely to him that whoever wanted him dead

41

might try again, once they heard that this ambush had failed.

He stepped over the corpse, trying to avoid stepping in blood as much as possible, and gathered up his rifle and saddlebags. By the time he had settled his hat on his head and gone back out into the hall again, the proprietor of the Pecos House was there waiting for him.

"Marshal, I'm so sorry about all this," the man began.

"Reckon I'm the one who ought to be apologizing," Longarm said. "Blood's mighty hard to get up off a floor and I reckon that bedspread in there is plumb ruined."

The hotel owner waved his hands back and forth. "No, no, don't worry about that. Are you all right? Were you hurt?"

"Nope. All I lost was a bottle of Maryland rye. It busted when I heaved it at those two gents. Made 'em duck, though, and that bought me a second or two."

"You can have another room, of course," the proprietor offered. "At no charge, naturally. And the hotel will replace that bottle of whiskey, too."

"That's mighty nice of you," Longarm allowed. "If you'll point out the room you want me to use . . ."

"Of course. Follow me."

The hotel man took Longarm down the corridor to another room and unlocked the door. Just then, at the other end of the hall, Dewey and the undertaker arrived and the young sheriff started shooing away the curious onlookers.

Longarm tossed his saddlebags on the bed and leaned his Winchester in a corner, then assured the proprietor that he didn't need anything else. "I'll have that bottle of whiskey sent up as soon as it gets here," the man promised.

Longarm nodded and closed the door behind him. Then he scaled his Stetson onto the bed next to the saddlebags and found another cheroot in his pocket. In all the excitement, he had dropped the one he'd been smoking when the shooting started. He didn't have any idea what had happened to it. Probably stomped to bits in all the gallivanting back and forth.

The hotel man had lit the lamp when he showed Longarm into the room. Now Longarm blew it out, pushed back the curtain over the window, and looked out at the street. This room was at the front of the hotel, so he had a good view of Fort Stockton. The street seemed a little busier than it had earlier. Probably more people were out and about because of the shooting. It must have sounded like a small war.

Longarm was still chewing on the unlit cheroot and thinking about what had happened when a knock sounded softly on the door. He turned away from the window and put his hand on the butt of his Colt. He figured his visitor was probably the proprietor or the desk clerk with that bottle of Tom Moore, but he wasn't going to take any chances.

"Who is it?"

"Harriet Summers," came the quiet-voiced reply.

Longarm frowned. He felt both relief and suspicion. He was glad to know that Harriet was all right and hadn't run afoul of the bushwhackers. But he still wondered if she'd had anything to do with the ambush.

There was one way to find out, he told himself.

He moved over to the door, turned the key in the lock, and stepped back quickly, his hand still hovering over the revolver. "It's open," he called.

The knob turned and the door swung toward him. He saw Harriet's shapely figure silhouetted against the light from the landing. As far as he could tell, she didn't have a gun or anything else in her hands. She stepped into the room and eased the door closed behind her.

"Hello, Custis," she said. "Are you all right? I heard there was some trouble."

Enough moonlight came through the window for him to be able to see her as she leaned back against the door. He couldn't read the expression on her face, though. She sounded genuinely worried about him, but that could have been an act.

"You must've heard the shooting," he said.

"Yes, of course. I didn't know you were involved, though, until I saw a crowd of men behind the hotel. I went back there to go up the rear stairs, as we planned. But when I saw there was some sort of trouble—Sheriff Arquette was back there, along with the undertaker and some of his men—I came back around to the front and went into the lobby. That's where I overheard some men talking about how someone tried to kill you."

"Two fellas bushwhacked me as I was going into my room," he confirmed. "I was lucky enough to live through it. They weren't."

He saw a small shudder go through her. "I knew your job must be more dangerous than you were letting on. Who were they? Why did they try to kill you?"

Longarm shook his head. "Don't know either of them things. I never saw the hombres before and they were a mite too dead to do any talking." He changed the subject by saying, "How'd you know where I was?"

"I heard Mr. Dempsey tell the clerk to get a bottle of Maryland rye and bring it up to you. He gave the clerk the number of your new room."

Dempsey was the owner of the Pecos House. Longarm figured the gent should have been a little more discreet than to announce the number of the room he'd moved into, considering that one attempt on his life had already been made tonight. Still, the fella probably hadn't suspected Harriet of spying on him.

"I'm surprised you showed up, knowing what happened," Longarm said. "Ain't you worried there'll be more trouble and you'll be caught in it next time?"

"I thought about going back to the fort," she admitted. "Uncle Dan and I have quarters behind the sutler's store.

But . . . I really wanted to see you, Custis. I had to make sure you were all right."

Or make sure those hired guns hadn't implicated her before they died, Longarm thought. That was a possibility, too.

"I'm fine," he assured her. "I reckon if you want, you can head on back to the fort now."

"I thought we were going to have a drink." She sounded disappointed.

"The fella ain't back yet with the whiskey."

"Well . . ." She reached behind her back. "If you'll come over here and help me undo the buttons on this dress, I'm sure we can find some way to pass the time until he gets here."

Chapter 6

For a moment, Longarm didn't move. As prim and re-served as Harriet had acted earlier in the day, she was be-having unusually boldly tonight. Ever since right after their dinner, she had made it plain that she intended to get him into bed with her.

Normally, Longarm didn't mind that at all. He had al-ways preferred women who spoke their minds and didn't behave like coy, simpering little idiots. He knew good and well that most gals had the same appetites and desires as men and he liked a woman who was willing to satisfy those appetites and desires.

But something didn't ring true about Harriet Summers. Several somethings, in fact. If he took her into his bed, would she try to kill him?

On several occasions in the past, he had bedded women who turned out to be cold-blooded killers. Sometimes the only way to uncover a plan was to play along with it. That made for a dangerous game.

"Well?" Harriet said a little impatiently as she flipped open the buttons she could reach. "Are you going to help me or not, Custis?"

"Turn around," he said as he moved closer to her, making up his mind.

She turned so that her back was to him. In the moonlight, he saw her lift her hair so that he could get to the top of the row of buttons that ran down the back of the dress. He undid the catch and unbuttoned the buttons, then spread the dress open as she let her hair fall again. She started to turn toward him again.

"Just stay like that," Longarm told her, his forceful tone brooking no argument.

"Oh. All right."

She stood there as he pulled the dress off her shoulders and then pushed it down around her waist. It slid over her hips and fell around her feet. She wore no corset underneath the dress. Her figure was so trim she didn't need one.

Longarm stepped closer to her, so close that he could smell the fragrance of her hair. He ran his hands over her body, caressing her through the thin, silken underthings. After stroking her thighs and hips, he slipped his arms around her and brought his hands up to cup her breasts. The globes of female flesh weren't overly large, but they were firm and rode high and proud on her chest. He filled his palms with them and thumbed the erect nipples through her undergarments.

"Oh, Custis, that feels so good," she breathed. Her head was tipped back with pleasure now. She pressed her buttocks back against his groin and rotated them sensuously.

She felt mighty good to him, too . . . and not the least of her appeal was that so far he hadn't found any weapons hidden on her.

Slowly, he stripped the rest of the clothes from her. She might have thought he was taking his time so as to draw out the pleasure of undressing her and to tell the truth, there was something to that. But he was being careful, too. It didn't take much room to hide a dagger or a derringer or a vial of poison.

Within a fairly short time, though, he had her nude, with a pile of clothes at her feet. She still had her back turned toward him. He massaged her shoulders and kissed the back of her neck, then rubbed her shoulder blades and moved on down to the small of her back. She leaned forward and put her hands on the wall to brace herself as he knelt behind her and kneaded the firm roundness of her derriere. Her thighs parted instinctively, allowing him to slip a hand between her legs and find the heated wetness of her core.

He still didn't trust her completely, but her arousal was genuine. There was no doubt about that, he thought as he stroked the slick folds of her femininity and then slipped a finger inside her. She gasped in pleasure at the penetration. Longarm added a second finger. Her muscles clasped him tightly.

Another knock sounded on the door. "Marshal Long?" the desk clerk's voice asked.

Harriet groaned.

"Marshal?"

"Hang on just a minute, old son," Longarm said quickly. He was still fully dressed, so all he had to do was take his fingers out of Harriet and step over to the door. With the lamp off, the clerk wouldn't be able to see much in the room, especially if Longarm didn't open the door very far.

He turned the knob and pulled the door about six inches toward him. The clerk stood there in the hall with a bottle of Tom Moore in his hands.

"I've got that rye for you, Marshal," the man said. "Compliments of the Pecos House."

"I'm much obliged," Longarm said as he reached out to take the bottle.

The clerk didn't give it to him immediately. "Do you need a glass? I'd be glad to—"

"Nope, no glass. This is fine," Longarm assured him. He practically grabbed the bottle out of the clerk's hands.

"Oh. All right, then." The man summoned up a smile

and nodded. "Good night. I hope there's no more trouble."

"You and me both, old son," Longarm said. He closed the door.

When he turned around, he saw that Harriet had slipped silently into the bed. The sheet was pulled up around her neck as she watched him in the moonlight.

"I feel positively scandalous," she whispered. "It's been so long since I've done anything like this."

"You've visited fellas in their hotel rooms before?"

He would have sworn that he could see her blushing, even in the shadows. "A lady's personal business is just that, Custis . . . personal."

"Can't argue with that," Longarm said. He came over to the bed and set the bottle on the night table. "You want that drink now?"

"Later," she breathed huskily. "Right now I want you out of those clothes."

That sounded pretty good to Longarm, too. The only problem was that his caution in making sure she didn't have any concealed weapons had been ruined by the clerk's untimely arrival. She could have grabbed something out of her clothes while his back was turned.

That was a chance he would just have to take, he told himself as he started taking off his clothes.

Harriet threw back the sheet, revealing that she was still completely nude. She got up on her knees to help him get rid of his clothes. Her hands went to his belt and the buttons of his fly while he was taking off his coat and vest and shirt. When his trousers were unfastened she pushed them down around his ankles, then hooked her fingers in the waistband of the bottom half of the long underwear and pulled it down, too. He was already erect and as his shaft came free it jutted out proudly from his groin, almost hitting her in the face. She wrapped her hands around the long, thick pole, gasping in surprise at its heft.

"My God, Custis!" she said. "I never expected this

50

much. I don't know if I can take it all." She laughed wickedly. "But I certainly intend to try!"

With that, she leaned over and began to lick around the head of his shaft. After a moment she opened her mouth wide and sucked it in.

She spoke fluent French. Just dandy, in fact. Longarm buried his hands in her thick red hair and hung on as she swallowed more and more of his manhood. The heat of her oral caress was searing. She caught hold of his buttocks to steady herself as her head bobbed up and down on his stiff pole.

He would have emptied himself into the hot, wet cavern of her mouth if she had kept up what she was doing for much longer. But just as he thought he was building to a climax that he couldn't hold back, she lifted her head with a gasp and quickly turned around. She pulled a pillow over so that she could rest her head on it and knelt on all fours with her rump stuck high in the air. The moonlight was silvery on the pale flesh.

"Take me now, Custis," she pleaded. "Put it in me!"

Longarm obliged her. He brought the head of his shaft to her heated opening and with a surge of his hips plunged into her.

Harriet buried her head in the pillow to muffle the cry of passion that welled up her throat. Longarm pumped in and out of her, launching into the timeless rhythm of man and woman joining as one. He held on tightly to her hips, bracing her so that the power of his thrusts wouldn't shove her across the bed. Deeper and deeper he plowed into her and it seemed that his manhood grew even longer and harder, although he didn't see how that was possible.

Even though a part of his brain remained alert for any danger, excitement rose in him until he was carried away by it. The rest of the world went away, until there was nothing but this room, this bed and the two of them and the slick, searing heat that they shared.

Longarm was too aroused to hold back. He drove in and out of her at an ever-increasing pace. She cried out again and thrust her hips back at him, taking in everything he had to give her. He felt a shudder go deeply through her as her culmination gripped her. That was enough to make his own climax boil up. His groin slammed against her buttocks as he stroked into her one last time and then froze with the entire length of his shaft buried as deeply inside her as it would go. He groaned as his seed spurted out, splashing hotly into her.

Once he reached that crest he seemed to stay there for an eternity before he started the long, slow, sweet slide down the other side. His chest heaved as he tried to catch his breath. A fine sheen of sweat covered his muscular body. With his manhood still throbbing inside her, he rubbed her back and hips. She was breathing heavily, too, as she knelt there in front of him.

When he finally pulled out of her, she toppled onto her side as if every muscle in her body had gone limp. He wondered for a second if she had actually passed out. But then she sighed and said, "Custis, that was wonderful." She rolled onto her back and held her arms up to him in invitation.

He went to her, sprawling half on her and half on the bed so that his weight wouldn't crush her. His arms went around her and drew her close to him. Their mouths met in a hot, searching kiss. Longarm realized that even though they had already made love, this was the first time they had kissed. That made it even more intimate and special.

She pulled her head back and said, "I'm shameless. I know that. I couldn't help myself. I tried to fight it, Custis, but the first time I saw you, I knew that I wanted you."

"I'm glad you didn't fight it too hard," Longarm said.

She stroked his back with her fingertips. "Don't think too badly of me," she whispered.

"For doing this?" he asked. "I don't think badly of you at all, Harriet. The world would be a better place if there was a heap more of this and a lot less hating and killing."

She pressed her face against his shoulder. "That's so true. Thank you, Custis."

Everything about her seemed sincere. He was almost ready to admit to himself that she hadn't had anything to do with the attempt on his life. Almost . . . but not quite. Not just yet.

The question remained: if she hadn't set up the ambush, who had? Who else in Fort Stockton had reason to want him dead?

Longarm had no idea and it seemed pretty doubtful that he would find out tonight. As Harriet's fingers closed around his manhood and began to caress and stroke the thick shaft back to life, it seemed even less likely.

Well, hell, he told himself, a man couldn't be suspicious *all* the time.

Despite that, when he finally went to sleep with her in his arms far into the night, he slept only lightly. His instincts would awaken him instantly if there was any sign of trouble.

He woke up in the morning when she slipped out of bed and started getting dressed. Propping himself up on an elbow, he said, "Your uncle's liable to be worried about you when he figures out you were gone all night."

She smiled at him. "Are you afraid he'll come after you with a shotgun, since he's my only male relative?"

"He just might," Longarm said. "He struck me as a pretty feisty old pelican."

"Don't worry. Uncle Dan won't cause any trouble. For one thing, he was probably playing cards until very late and then I'm sure he went into his room and fell asleep right away. He's a very sound sleeper. It's early enough I can get back into my room without disturbing him."

Longarm frowned. "The soldiers at the fort will know you're coming in, though. Damn it, Harriet, I never meant to hurt your reputation."

She came over to the bed with her dress still unbuttoned and bent down to kiss him. Then she turned around and said, "You're very sweet, Custis, but you don't have to worry about me. I'm a grown woman, after all. Just help me with these buttons, will you?"

He stood up, still naked, and fastened the buttons. Harriet turned to face him again, came up on her toes, brushed her lips across his, and reached down to give his pecker a fond squeeze.

"Thank you," she whispered. "You don't know what last night meant to me."

Longarm could have held her, but he sensed that she wanted to go. He didn't try to stop her. She smiled at him and then slipped out the door, moving quickly but quietly. He glanced at the window. The light outside was still gray. It was barely dawn. She might be able to get out of the hotel and back to the fort before too many people were out and about.

As he turned back toward the bed, he saw her spectacles sitting on the night table next to the lamp. He supposed she had set them there the night before when she'd slipped into the bed. They had never gotten around to drinking any of that Maryland rye. The unopened bottle still sat on the table, too.

Longarm picked up the spectacles and turned toward the door. He thought about opening it and seeing if Harriet was still in the hall. But then he stopped. He didn't want to call her name or cause any commotion that might embarrass her. He would have to stop by the fort and talk to Colonel Bascomb again before he rode out on the trail of that missing patrol. He could give the spectacles to Harriet then. From what he had observed, she didn't really need them all that much.

In fact, he saw as he lifted the spectacles to his eyes and peered through the lenses, she didn't need them at all. He had just confirmed something he had suspected the night before, when he had looked into her eyes while they were at the restaurant.

The spectacles were nothing but clear glass, just like looking through a window.

Chapter 7

The Pecos House had a small dining room. Longarm was sitting at a table in it, sipping coffee and having breakfast, when Sheriff Dewey Arquette came in. Longarm could tell from the way Dewey came straight toward him that the young lawman had been looking for him.

"Pull up a chair," Longarm invited as Dewey walked up to the table. "There's plenty of coffee in the pot."

"Don't mind if I do," Dewey said as he took a seat across the table. He motioned to a black-jacketed waiter to bring him a cup.

"Want some breakfast, Sheriff?" the waiter asked as he placed a clean cup and saucer in front of Dewey.

"No, this'll do fine, Clyde. Thanks." Dewey poured himself a cup, sipped the strong black brew appreciatively, and then said, "No more trouble last night?"

Longarm thought about the time he had spent with Harriet Summers and said, "No trouble."

But there was still the mystery of those clear-glass spectacles and why Harriet would wear them when she didn't need them.

"Well, nobody in town seems to know those two hard-cases who came after you. I asked around and nobody would admit to ever seeing them before."

"That don't mean much," Longarm pointed out. "Men drift in and out all the time, I expect."

Dewey nodded. "That's true and I wouldn't be surprised if some of the bartenders in the dives on the edge of town had seen them. Nobody in those places likes to talk to the law."

"Well, I wouldn't worry about it. At least they had enough money on 'em to pay for the county to bury them."

"Blood money, you mean," Dewey said.

"Yeah, but it weren't my blood that got spilled. Reckon that's where their plan got a mite fouled up."

Dewey nodded and they sat in companionable silence for several minutes while Longarm cleaned up the last of his flapjacks, hash browns, and eggs. He had already polished off the thick steak that had come with the breakfast.

A boy in a floppy-brimmed hat came into the dining room, looked around, and then started toward the table when he spotted Longarm and Dewey. "Marshal Long?" he asked as he came up.

"That's me, son," Longarm replied. "What can I do for you?"

"Mr. Bradley over at the telegraph office sent me to look for you." The youngster pulled out a folded envelope. "Said for me to give you this when I found you."

Longarm took the envelope and dug a coin out of his pocket. He flipped it to the boy, who caught it deftly. "Much obliged," Longarm told him.

The boy bit the coin, probably out of habit to see if it was real, then hesitated beside the table.

"Was there something else you needed?" Longarm asked.

"I was just wonderin' . . . You killed them two fellas who ambushed you last night, didn't you, Marshal?"

Longarm nodded solemnly. "I did. Pretty much had to."

"Could I touch you for luck?"

Longarm frowned. "Luck?"

"Yes, sir. You're still alive, so I reckon you must be a pretty lucky man. I'm hopin' some of it will rub off."

Dewey leaned forward. "Quit botherin' the marshal and run along now."

Longarm lifted a hand and said, "No, that's all right." To the youngster he went on, "I don't much hold with touching a fella for luck, but I'll tell you what I'll do. I'd be glad to shake your hand, son, in thanks for bringing me that message."

"Really?" the youngster said, wide-eyed. "Thanks, Marshal."

Still solemn, Longarm shook hands with the boy, who hurried out to tell his friends about his encounter with a famous lawman.

"I didn't know he was goin' to pester you like that," Dewey said.

"Don't worry about it," Longarm assured him. "What that young fella don't know is that he's gone and misplaced his hero worship. Ain't nothing special about me. I'm just a lawman, going about his job."

"If it was anybody else, Marshal, I'd say that was false modesty. But I know you mean it."

Longarm snorted. "Damn right I do." He tore open the envelope. "Let's see what this has got to say."

As he expected, the message was from Billy Vail. It was short and to the point, as Vail always was, and authorized Longarm to investigate the disappearance of the missing cavalry patrol from Fort Stockton. Longarm turned the telegram around and pushed it across the table so that Dewey could read it.

The sheriff scanned the message and then glanced up at Longarm. "I've heard rumors about a patrol riding out and not coming back to the fort. I wasn't sure it was true, though. Colonel Bascomb is pretty close-mouthed when it comes to army matters."

"Yeah. He didn't tell me that his soldiers helped with the search for that outlaw gang, either."

Dewey frowned. "You reckon the two things might be connected, Marshal?" He tapped a fingertip on the telegram. "If that patrol happened to run across those owlhoots . . . or even worse, if they rode into an ambush . . ."

"The same thing occurred to me," Longarm said. "Could be we've got a bunch of murdered soldier boys out there somewhere."

"Damn," Dewey muttered. "When the outlaws make war on the army . . ."

"Somebody's got to round them up. I'll make a start on it. I may need help before it's over, though."

"Anything I can do, Marshal, you just let me know. I want this mess cleaned up as much as you do."

Longarm drank the last of his coffee and then pushed his chair back. "I'd better go by the store and stock up on supplies," he said as he got to his feet. "No telling how long I'll be on the trail. Then I'll go by the fort and talk to Colonel Bascomb before I ride out."

Dewey stood up and shook hands with him. "Good luck, Marshal."

Longarm grinned and said, "Reckon I'll probably need it. Let's just hope that youngster didn't get all my luck a while ago."

He went to the livery stable first and picked up his horse, then rode down to the general store and went inside to buy food and ammunition. He still had the unopened bottle of whiskey, which he stashed away in his saddlebags. A fella never knew when something like that would come in handy . . . strictly for medicinal purposes, of course. He smiled when he thought of Harriet saying that.

From there he went to the fort. The guard on duty recognized him and sent him right to the headquarters building. When Longarm went inside, he found Major Ordway seated at one of the desks in the outer office. The adjutant started to get up from the other desk, but Ordway said, "I'll handle this, Corporal." To Longarm, he went on, "Have you come to see Colonel Bascomb, Marshal?"

Longarm nodded. "That's right."

"You must have heard from Marshal Vail in Denver."

Longarm didn't answer for a second. His business was with Colonel Bascomb, not Major Ordway, but from what he had seen the day before, the colonel didn't keep any secrets from his second-in-command. Longarm knew, too, how fast and efficiently the army grapevine worked.

"Yeah, I did," he replied.

"I'll take you to the colonel," Ordway said. He knocked on the door of the inner office and when Bascomb answered, he said, "Marshal Long here to see you, sir."

"Well, bring him in!" Bascomb called. Ordway stepped back to usher Longarm through the door first.

Longarm nodded to the colonel and got right down to business. "I've heard from my boss."

Bascomb motioned for Ordway to close the door and stay in the office. "Go on, Marshal," he said. "I hope the news is good."

"Depends on how you look at it," Longarm said. "Marshal Vail agreed that I ought to see if I can find that missing patrol for you."

Bascomb looked relieved. "I was hoping that was what you'd say."

"Me, too. I got to admit, I'm more than a mite curious about what could have happened to those troopers of yours."

Bascomb stood up and extended a hand across the desk. "Thank you, Marshal," he said fervently. "If there's anything the army can do to help you, just let me know."

Longarm shook the colonel's hand and said, "I wouldn't mind hearing anything you can tell me about a gang of outlaws that's been raiding all over West Texas for the past year."

61

Bascomb frowned as he released Longarm's hand. "You heard about that?"

"Sheriff Arquette mentioned it. He even said that some of your boys had helped him look for those owlhoots."

"Yes, that's true," Bascomb said with a sigh. "I should have said something about it, I suppose, but to tell you the truth, Marshal, I didn't think there was any connection. You see, I don't believe there *is* such a gang."

That comment made Longarm frown. "The sheriff seemed mighty sure of it."

"Oh, I don't doubt that the robberies and such have taken place. Where I think the sheriff makes his mistake is in assuming that one particular group of outlaws is responsible for all of them."

"You're saying you believe different bunches are pulling off the jobs?"

Bascomb looked at Ordway and the major spoke up. "That's the way it appears, Marshal. I was in charge of the effort to locate the outlaws and I made a study of the crimes. They're simply too far-flung and too varied in nature to have been the work of a single group. Not only that, but I'm convinced that if that really were the case, the outlaws would have been discovered and captured by now."

"But you helped look for them," Longarm pointed out.

"We try to cooperate with the local authorities," Bascomb said. "Our real duty here at this post is to protect the settlers from Indians and from incursions by Mexican insurgents who come up from below the border to raid. But we're willing to help out with criminal matters when we can."

"On one occasion," Ordway went on, "Lieutenant Morgan and his men rode into a settlement right after outlaws had robbed the bank. He found the trail and gave chase, but the men vanished, and so did their trail. It's my opinion that they all split up. They probably work as ranch hands in the area."

"Maybe," Longarm said. He wasn't convinced, though.

He knew Dewey Arquette, knew that the young man had grown well into the job of sheriff. If Dewey laid the blame for the series of depredations at the feet of one gang, then Longarm was inclined to believe him, no matter what these army officers said.

"I apologize if you think I misled you, Marshal," Bascomb said. "It's been several months since my men were involved in the search for this so-called gang, and it honestly just didn't occur to me that there might be a connection."

"Well, I reckon we'll see," Longarm said. "Which way was the patrol headed when it left here?"

"South toward the Big Bend," Ordway said, standing by one of the maps on the wall and pointing. "They were to loop down close to the river and then return to the fort by way of Marfa and Alpine."

Longarm nodded. He knew both of those settlements. They hadn't been in existence for too long, but they were growing steadily because of nearby ranches and the Texas & New Orleans Railroad, which had reached the area just north of the Big Bend a couple of years earlier.

"I'll see what I can find," he promised. He shook hands again with both officers and left the headquarters building.

There was just one more errand he had to take care of before he rode out of Fort Stockton. Leading his horse, he walked over to the sutler's store. Several troopers stood on the porch and nodded to him as he came up the steps.

Longarm returned the nods and moved on into the dim interior of the store. A man wearing a canvas apron stood behind a counter at the rear. "Help you, mister?" he said as Longarm came toward him.

"I'm looking for Miss Summers." Longarm reached toward his shirt pocket, where he had put the spectacles he'd found in the hotel room this morning. "I've got something for her."

"She's not here," the sutler said with a frown and a shake of his head.

"I thought she keeps your books and lives in quarters behind the store."

"She does, but I haven't seen her this morning."

Longarm felt a pang of worry. Maybe Harriet had run into some trouble while she was walking back to the fort in the predawn gloom. Somebody could have jumped her and carried her off. It was very rare on the frontier for any man, even the most snake-blooded of hard cases, to bother a woman, but it happened from time to time.

"What about her uncle? He doesn't know where she might be?"

"That old-timer?" Again the sutler shook his head. "He's gone, too. There's no sign of either one of them."

Now Longarm's suspicions kicked in again, to go with his worries. If Uncle Dan had disappeared, too, there was a good chance he was with Harriet, wherever she was. Maybe dropping out of sight had been their idea. There seemed to be a lot of it going around . . . an outlaw gang that vanished, a cavalry patrol that rode out and never came back, and now a beautiful young woman and her great-uncle had up and disappeared, too.

There *had* to be a connection, Longarm thought.

And now, with Harriet gone, too, and maybe in danger, he had more reason than ever to find out what it was.

Chapter 8

Longarm rode south, the shallow valley of the Pecos River to his left, the low and rounded Glass Mountains off to the right. Far to the southwest, he could see the Santiagos, which led down into the Big Bend country, so called because of the giant curve that the Rio Grande made. Eventually the Santiagos turned into the Chisos Mountains, some of the most rugged country to be found in Texas. The Big Bend was large enough and wild enough to hide a lot of things . . .

Including a gang of outlaws, a missing cavalry patrol, and a girl and an old man?

Longarm didn't know, but he intended to find out.

Other than the mountains in the distance, the landscape was mostly flat, dotted with yucca and scrub brush and a very occasional tree. There was enough grass to support the hardy breeds of cattle that populated West Texas ranches, but it took a lot of acres to graze one cow, which explained why the spreads were so large. A small rancher had no chance in this part of the country.

An exceptionally stubborn farmer might make a go of it, though, and Longarm passed a few such places, with fields irrigated from the Pecos River or one of the winding creeks that fed into it and worked by Mexican peons in white clothes, wide-brimmed sombreros, and rope sandals.

Some of them stopped their labors long enough to wave to Longarm as he rode past and he returned the waves with a grin. Nobody was friendlier or more hospitable than these farmers. They would feed a man and give him a place to sleep, and never expect anything in return.

Colonel Bascomb had said that no one in the settlement of Marathon had seen the missing patrol. Marathon was several days' ride south of Fort Stockton, so it seemed likely that the patrol had veered off from the main road before reaching the settlement. Longarm kept a close eye on both sides of the trail. Several weeks had passed, normally long enough for wind and weather to wipe out any hoof-prints, but Longarm knew from talking to Dewey Arquette that it hadn't rained during that time. The West Texas wind blew pretty much all the time, but some tracks might be left anyway. Sixteen riders in a bunch would leave quite a bit of sign.

Several trails branched off from the main road. Longarm checked the ones he came to during the first day and didn't see any tracks that would indicate the patrol had taken them, or any signs that they had headed off across open country.

He spent the first night at one of the farms he passed. It was owned by a family named Zapata. They made him welcome and he rode on the next morning with his belly full from a good breakfast of tortillas and beans and strong black coffee.

He'd had a day to think about it, to mull over all the possibilities, and he wasn't a bit closer to any answers than he had been when he left Fort Stockton. His lawman's instincts told him that all the puzzles he had run across had some common pieces, but he was damned if he could fit them together.

Some dark clouds began to form in the sky above a

butte to the west that Longarm knew was called Panther Mesa. Thunder rumbled and lightning flickered in those clouds, even though where Longarm was the sun was still shining and the air was hot.

Rainstorms were few and far between in these parts, but on the rare occasions when a cloud came up, the result could be a real gullywasher. Not only that, but sometimes those storms could spawn cyclones. More than one little West Texas community had been completely blown away by tornadoes.

So Longarm kept a close eye on those clouds to the west. After a while, he saw gray sheets of rain falling from them. The rain wasn't reaching the ground, though. Like the ragged bottom edge of a curtain, the rain ended while it was still high in the sky.

Longarm knew the air below the clouds was so dry that the raindrops dried right up when they hit it. He had seen such things before and little quirks of nature like that made him glad his job kept him outdoors most of the time. He reckoned he would go plumb crazy if he had to sit in a building all day, every day.

The wind freshened and was actually a little cool. It felt good. The clouds crept farther east and blocked the sun, casting welcome shadows over the parched ground.

Longarm frowned, torn between two emotions. The coolness was a welcome relief, but if a hard rain actually started, it could wipe out the tracks he was searching for. Hoofprints were more durable than most folks gave them credit for, but a hard enough downpour would still erase them.

The road curved closer to the mesa. Longarm cast a worried glance at the black, scudding clouds as more thunder rumbled and it was while he was looking up at the sky that he felt as much as heard something whip past his ear.

He knew instantly that a bullet had just narrowly missed him. Hunching forward in the saddle, he jabbed his heels into the roan's flanks and sent the horse leaping ahead in a gallop. Lightning smashed down a mile or so away and this time the thunder was a deafening roar.

With so much racket going on, he couldn't hear the shots. But as he saw dust spurt up in the roadway just ahead of him, he knew somebody was still shooting at him. Unfortunately, there was no cover along this stretch of the trail. All he could do was ride hell-for-leather and try to get out of range before the bushwhacker could draw a bead on him.

The roan jumped suddenly and let out a shrill whinny. Longarm saw blood on the horse's withers where a bullet had nicked it. The wound was a shallow one, but it hurt enough so that the roan was spooked. The horse stopped galloping and started bucking frenziedly.

Back in his cowboying days when he had first come west after the war, Longarm had busted many a bronc, so he knew how to sit a saddle even when the horse went to twisting and sunfishing. He hung on for dear life, knowing that if nothing else the bushwhacker would have a hard time hitting him as long as he was on the back of a crazy, bucking horse.

Cowboys sometimes had competitions among themselves to see who could stay on a bucking bronc the longest. Longarm had no idea how long he perched there on the roan's back as the horse plunged and leaped madly across the prairie, but it seemed like an eternity. The wild ride came to an abrupt halt, however, when the roan stepped in a prairie dog hole and went down.

Longarm kicked his feet free of the stirrups as the horse started to fall. He threw himself out of the saddle, not wanting the roan to land on him and pin him down, maybe even bust his leg. Hoping he wouldn't land in a clump of prickly pear, he put his hands out to break his fall.

He came down hard but was able to roll a couple of times and spend some of his momentum that way. His hat went flying off. He wound up on his belly and as he raised his head to look around, another bullet smacked into the ground not far away, throwing dust and grit into his face and half blinding him.

Blinking his eyes rapidly, he rolled to the side again, unwilling to give the bushwhacker a stationary target. He reached down to his holster, clawing for the Colt even though he knew the range was probably too great for a handgun.

Empty. The revolver must have fallen out when he hit the ground.

And his Winchester was in the saddle boot on the roan, which had struggled back to its feet and was now dancing away skittishly, at least twenty yards down the trail.

Well, it was official, thought Longarm. Even here in mostly dry West Texas, he was up Shit Creek.

But he couldn't just lie there, bury his face in the sand, and hope that the bushwhacker wouldn't hit him. That was a good way to wind up dead in a hurry. Although it seemed like an unnatural thing to do, he had to draw even more fire, in hopes of discovering where the rifleman was shooting from.

He surged to his feet and broke into a run, heading toward the roan just in case the horse might let him get his hands on his Winchester. The roan veered away before he could get close, though.

Letting his instincts guide him, Longarm zigged and zagged, running a path as jagged as the lightning that clawed through the black clouds above the mesa. A bullet kicked up dirt at his heels.

The closest good cover was a cluster of rocks at the base of the mesa. He ran toward them, still angling from side to side in a crazy pattern. Another slug smacked past his ear and this time he saw a puff of smoke from among the rocks. His guess had been right. That was where the bushwhacker was holed up.

Longarm flung himself to the ground as another bullet burned through the air just above his head. A second later and the lead would have driven right into his chest. He rolled and suddenly spotted what he had been looking for: a dry wash that twisted across the landscape toward the mesa.

He wasn't completely unarmed. The little .41 caliber derringer was in his pocket. Its range was so short, though, that he would have to be mighty close to use it.

That wash might be just what he needed to get him close enough. He scrambled toward it and dived in just as another slug hit the ground near him. The bushwhacker was persistent, whoever he was.

More grit showered around Longarm as the rifleman peppered the edge of the wash with slugs. The water-worn depression in the ground was just deep enough, though, to give the big lawman sufficient cover. It was a couple of yards wide and maybe two feet deep. By keeping his head down, Longarm could crawl along the wash toward the mesa in relative safety.

The shooting died away, but that didn't mean the bushwhacker was giving up. He could have realized the futility of trying to hit his target while Longarm was in the wash.

The wind began to blow harder and now it carried with it the smell of the rain. Longarm glanced up as he crawled. As the storm approached, some of the rain appeared to be reaching the top of the mesa. A moment later, a big drop plopped into the sand in front of his face.

If it rained hard enough, the wash would start running with water. Wouldn't it be a hell of a note, he thought, if he drowned in the middle of this arid landscape?

Maybe it wouldn't come to that. He was squirming along as fast as he could and still keep his head down.

The rain began to pelt down from the heavens. Lightning popped and crackled, followed almost instantly by booming peals of thunder. Longarm risked a glance and saw that the mesa was no longer visible. It was hidden by blinding sheets of rain.

If he couldn't see the mesa—and the cluster of boulders at its base—that meant the bushwhacker hidden there couldn't see him, either. Realizing that, Longarm leaped up, bounded out of the shallow wash, and charged toward the spot where he thought the mesa was.

A moment later the rocky upthrust of ground loomed out of the gray shroud of the downpour. Longarm slowed down and advanced more cautiously. He was soaked to the skin after only a few minutes of rain. The fat drops pounded him like thousands of tiny fists.

He slipped his hand inside his pocket and closed it around the derringer. The little two-shot pistol fired metallic cartridges, of course, so the rain wouldn't have any effect on it. He still needed to get closer, though. He stole toward the rocks.

Then he was among them and he paused to listen, hoping to hear some sound that would give away the position of the bushwhacker. He couldn't hear anything except the wind and the rain and the thunder. Pressing his back against a boulder, Longarm slid around it, holding the derringer ready. He blinked his eyes in an attempt to keep the water out of them.

Suddenly a dark shape, gigantic in the rain, came around the rock toward him. Longarm lurched away from it before he realized it was a horse.

"Son of a bitch!"

The startled exclamation came from the man leading the horse, reins clutched in one hand while the other held a rifle. Longarm knew he had found the bushwhacker . . . or rather, he and the bushwhacker had found each other.

The man dropped the reins and tried to jerk the rifle up. Longarm thrust the derringer at him and pulled the trigger. Only a few feet separated the lawman from the ambusher who had tried to kill him. The range was short enough for the derringer to be effective. It barked and spat flame.

71

The .41 caliber slug grazed the man's upper right arm and made him drop the rifle. He cursed again and grabbed awkwardly for the holstered revolver on his hip, but the wound slowed him down and made him clumsy. Longarm triggered the derringer's second shot.

This time the bullet ripped into the man's thigh and knocked him back a step. He slewed around sideways and started to fall.

But even as he went down, his left hand plucked a knife from a sheath on that hip and flicked it at Longarm. Longarm had to leap aside to keep the blade from burying itself in his chest.

That gave the bushwhacker time to catch his balance on one knee. With his wounded leg dragging behind him, he stubbornly dived forward, tackling Longarm around the knees. Grating a curse of his own, Longarm went down.

The bushwhacker scrambled up on hands and knees and threw a hard left fist. The blow smashed into Longarm's jaw and rocked his head to the side. He was stunned for a heartbeat, but he fought off the feeling and his hand shot up to fasten around his opponent's throat. Longarm rolled to the side, taking the bushwhacker with him.

Even with two bullet wounds, the man was like a wildcat. Longarm had his hands full. He managed to get on top and held on and got a second hand around the man's throat, even though the bushwhacker kept punching him left-handed. He bore down, hoping that the lack of air would cause the man to pass out.

Instead, the bushwhacker stopping hitting Longarm and flailed to the side with his good arm instead. Luck—good or bad, depending on how you looked at it—led his hand to fall on the handle of the knife he had tossed at Longarm a minute earlier. He closed his fingers around it and brought it up and around, slashing at Longarm's face.

Longarm saw the blade coming at him in time to throw himself backward and avoid it. Otherwise his throat would have been ripped open. He lost his grip on the bush-whacker in the process. Gasping for air, the man reared up and lunged at him again, swinging the knife.

Going low, Longarm let the blade pass over his head and reached up to grab the man's arm. He heaved and twisted, and the maneuver sent the bushwhacker rolling across the wet ground. He screamed in pain and surprise, and as he came to a stop lying on his back, Longarm saw the handle of the knife sticking up from his chest. The blade had gotten turned around somehow and as the man rolled over it, he had stabbed himself.

"Damn it, don't you die!" Longarm yelled as he threw himself at the bushwhacker. He wanted to know who had hired the man to try to kill him. He reached for the knife, intending to yank it out, but he was too late.

The shudder that went through the man and the rattle of a final breath in his throat told Longarm that he was dead.

Longarm pounded a fist in the mud in frustration. Even in the rain, he could see the bushwhacker's face well enough to know that the man was a stranger to him. That meant that more than likely he was another hired gun.

But who had hired him?

The question wasn't destined to be answered immediately. The sudden pounding of hoofbeats told Longarm that someone else was coming. With a snarl, the lawman snatched the Colt from the holster on the bushwhacker's hip and came up in a crouch, wheeling around to meet the new threat, whatever it was.

Chapter 9

"Whoa!" a voice called as the rider reined in. "Whoa!"

Surprise went through Longarm as he recognized the voice. The last time he'd heard it, it had been whispering affectionately to him. It belonged to Harriet Summers.

Despite what had happened between them and the un-expectedness of her showing up here on the scene of his battle with the bushwhacker, he hadn't forgotten his suspicions of her. He kept the gun leveled and covered the figure that was indistinct because of the downpour.

"Hold it!" he shouted, raising his voice enough to be heard over the thunder. "Don't try anything, Harriet!"

"Custis! Is that you?"

Longarm figured she knew good and well it was him.

"Harriet, what are you doing here?" he demanded. "Come ahead, but take it slow and easy."

She walked her horse toward him. As she came closer, he could see her well enough to tell that she wore trousers and rode astride, like a man. She wore a man's hat, too, a black, flat-crowned Stetson that was held on her head by a tight chin strap.

The man's shirt she wore was tight, too. Or maybe it just

looked that way because of the breasts thrusting out against the rain-soaked fabric.

"Custis, are you all right?" she asked as she brought the horse to a stop.

"I reckon."

"Who's that?" She gestured as she asked the question and he knew she was pointing at the dead man on the ground behind him.

He answered honestly, "I don't rightly know. Some hombre who wanted me dead; that's all I'm sure of."

Even in the rain, he could see the concern on her face. "You were ambushed again?"

"That's right. You know anything about it?"

The blunt question made her frown. She said, "Why would I know anything about it?"

"You disappear from Fort Stockton and then show up in the middle of nowhere, right after some fella I don't know starts taking potshots at me. It don't take a genius to think that there might be some connection."

Harriet shook her head and said, "I swear, Custis, I had nothing to do with this. As for everything else . . . well, I can explain it."

"Maybe you better start doing that," Longarm said coolly.

"All right, I—" The creaking of wagon wheels interrupted her. She looked behind her as Longarm stepped back and swung the revolver slightly to one side, so that he could cover whoever was in the wagon.

This time he wasn't surprised. A covered wagon being pulled by a team of four horses loomed up out of the rain, which had begun to taper off a little. These desert storms, fierce while they lasted, tended not to go on for too long. White-bearded Uncle Dan Boldin sat on the driver's seat of the wagon. With a shout to his team, he hauled back on the reins and brought the animals to a halt.

"Howdy, Marshal," he called. "You get elected?"

"No, but that hombre on the ground did his best to nominate me a heap of times," Longarm replied.

"Bushwhacker, eh?"

"That's right."

"You know him?"

"Never saw him before in my life."

Harriet said, "Just like the men who attacked you back in Fort Stockton. You obviously have some determined enemies, Custis."

"Yeah, and I wonder who they might be," Longarm said, looking meaningfully at Harriet and her great-uncle.

Uncle Dan drew himself up stiffly on the wagon seat. "What in thunderation!" he exclaimed. "Are you sayin' you think Harriet an' me had somethin' to do with this?"

"She says you didn't."

"And she's tellin' the truth, too! Why, hell, son, we came hurryin' along to help you when we heard that shootin'!"

"You've been following me?" Longarm snapped.

"Ever since you left Fort Stockton," Harriet replied.

"Why would you do a thing like that, if you're not up to no good?"

Harriet hesitated a moment before answering. She looked over at Uncle Dan, who nodded at her as if telling her to go ahead and answer the question honestly.

Harriet turned her gaze back to Longarm and said, "Because I think you have a chance of finding out what happened to that missing patrol, and if you do, I want to be there."

Longarm frowned. He had wondered if there was some connection between Harriet and the missing cavalrymen, but he hadn't expected her to come right out and admit it that easily. He asked, "What business is that of yours?"

"Officially, none, of course. But personally . . ." She hesitated again, then lifted her chin and plunged on. "I'm in love with Scott . . . Lieutenant Morgan. I . . . I have to find out what happened to him. And to the other men, of course."

Longarm couldn't help but stare at her as he remembered how enthusiastically and unashamedly she had made love with him a couple of nights earlier, only to declare now that she was in love with another man.

He was well aware, though, that what happened in bed between a man and a woman didn't always prevent her from feeling the same way about another man. Love was a complicated business and he had learned over the years not to pass judgment on anybody for following their heart.

"I knew that Colonel Bascomb asked for your help in locating the patrol," Harriet went on. "When I asked around about your reputation, I figured you had a chance to succeed where the others had failed."

"How did you find out what Bascomb asked me to do?"

Harriet smiled in the rain. "You know how hard it is to keep secrets on an army post, Custis. There are always rumors and gossip."

"And folks tend to talk more in front of an old geezer and a pretty girl," Uncle Dan put in with a laugh. "Ain't much goes on around that fort that we don't know about, Marshal."

What they were saying sounded reasonable. Longarm finally lowered the gun in his hand. "All right," he said. "I reckon maybe you didn't have anything to do with me being bushwhacked. But that don't mean I'm going to let you tag along while I look for those soldiers."

"But you have to!" Harriet exclaimed. "We can help you. Like I told you, when we heard those shots, we rushed right up here to see if there was anything we could do."

"I'm used to taking care of myself," Longarm said. He jerked his head toward the body of the bushwhacker. "Just like that."

"But what if you'd been pinned down?" she insisted. "We might have saved your life."

She couldn't know it, but she came pretty close to the mark with that notion, Longarm thought. He had almost been pinned down, just as she said. If that wash hadn't been nearby, there was a good chance he'd be dead by now.

Still, he was accustomed to working alone. Having to watch out for a young woman and an old pelican like Uncle Dan might prove to a serious hindrance to his plans. Not that he really *had* a plan at the moment . . .

"All right," he said with a sigh. "I reckon I could use a hand, at least for now. For one thing, my horse ran off, and I'll need some help catching him."

"I'll do that," Harriet said without hesitation. "I saw him running off a ways when I rode up." Without waiting for anything else, she wheeled her mount and urged it into a swift trot, riding off into the rain to look for Longarm's horse.

"She rides like she's used to the saddle," Longarm commented to Uncle Dan.

The old-timer snorted. "She durned sure ought to be. Practically growed up on horseback, she did. And wait'll you see her shoot!"

It would be all right with him if he never saw that, Longarm thought. He didn't like the idea of Harriet being mixed up in the sort of corpse-and-cartridge sessions that popped up during most of his assignments.

But he had a bad feeling that if she stuck with him, sooner or later that was exactly what was going to happen.

The rain stopped a short time later, and the menacing black clouds broke up and blew away, revealing the deep blue sky and the molten ball of the sun that shone down and started drying the puddles almost immediately. For a time, the air would hold the fresh, clean scent of the rain and the desert roses would bloom.

But by mid-afternoon, it was just hot and dry again, with even the memory of the rain gone from the baking landscape.

Longarm and Harriet rode alongside the wagon driven

by Uncle Dan. Harriet had caught Longarm's roan without much trouble, furnishing further proof that she knew how to handle herself in a saddle.

She had insisted that they bury the dead bushwhacker, even though Uncle Dan had grumbled that it was a waste of time and energy to plant such a polecat. Longarm went along with Harriet, despite the fact that if it had been up to him, he might have been inclined to let the buzzards and coyotes take care of the corpse, too.

"I figure Lieutenant Morgan and the rest of the patrol must've left the main trail somewhere between Fort Stockton and Marathon," he explained to Harriet as they rode south. "I've been watching for any signs of that, but so far I ain't come across any."

"And now, after that rain, any tracks will be washed out," she said.

Longarm shrugged. "You'd be surprised how long hoofprints will last, but yeah, I reckon a frog-strangler like the one that blew through earlier wiped out any sign that was left. We'll still keep an eye out."

They jogged along in silence for a few minutes, then Longarm said, "You must know that young lieutenant pretty well."

Harriet smiled. "Yes, I do."

"Did he seem bothered by anything before him and his men left on this last patrol?"

Harriet's smile went away and was replaced by a troubled frown. "Last patrol," she repeated. "I don't like the sound of that. It's so . . . final."

"That ain't really the way I meant it," he said. But he still strongly suspected that might turn out to be the case.

"To answer your question," Harriet said, "I didn't notice that Scott was upset about anything. He was a good young officer, eager to carry out his duty—" She stopped short. "*Was.* Now I'm doing it."

"We'll find him and the others," Longarm said. "West

Texas is a mighty big place, but sixteen cavalry troopers don't just up and disappear."

"I hope you're right."

By nightfall they still hadn't reached Marathon and had not found any tracks that indicated the patrol had left the trail. Not finding a farm where they could spend the night, Longarm said, "I reckon we'll just have to pull off the road a ways and make camp."

"Harriet can sleep in the wagon," Uncle Dan said. "I don't mind throwin' my bedroll underneath it. That's what we did last night."

Longarm located a suitable spot, venturing off the trail to find a clearing in a thick stand of mesquite and chaparral. The top of the wagon would still be visible from the road, but at least they would have a little protection if anyone came looking for trouble.

After everything that had happened, Longarm sure wasn't going to rule out that possibility.

Harriet made a small fire from mesquite branches while Longarm and Uncle Dan tended to the horses, then the old-timer announced that he would take care of fixing supper.

"Gal can't cook worth a flip," he said with an affectionate grin at Harriet, who stuck her tongue out at him. Longarm wouldn't have expected such a girlish reaction from her, given her generally serious nature, but he was coming to realize that Harriet Summers was full of surprises.

While Uncle Dan got busy with beans and bacon and biscuits, Longarm took his rifle and walked back out to the road to make sure no one was on their back trail. Harriet went with him.

"I'm a little surprised you let us come with you," she said quietly. "I thought you'd send us back, since we're still relatively close to Fort Stockton."

"Don't think I didn't consider it," he said. "I still ain't sure you ought to be out here. If I sent you back, though, would you really go? Or would you just pretend to and start trailing me again?"

She laughed softly. "Are you saying that you brought us along just so that you can keep an eye on us?"

"Something like that," Longarm admitted.

She grew more solemn. "You still don't trust me, do you?"

Longarm broached the subject that he had mulled over earlier. "A couple of nights ago you didn't act much like a gal who was pining away for a lost love."

She stopped and as he came to a halt, too, and turned to face her, for a second he thought she was going to slap him.

"You have no right to say that," she told him in a voice husky with emotion. "You don't know the strain I've been under since . . . since Scott disappeared. And I'll admit, I'm no blushing virgin. I wasn't when I came to Fort Stockton. When I saw you . . . I was drawn to you, Custis. I admit that. Under the circumstances, I probably shouldn't have acted on those feelings." She lifted her chin. "I can promise you, it won't happen again."

Her anger seemed genuine. Longarm was sorry she wasn't interested in any more romping with him, but the way things stood now, that was probably for the best. He had to concentrate on the job that had brought him here . . .

He turned his head sharply toward the road as he heard the pounding of hoofbeats. A lot of hoofbeats. A large group of riders was approaching.

He put a hand on Harriet's shoulder and said, "Get down behind that mesquite. Don't show yourself."

"Who do you think they are?" she asked a little breathlessly.

"I don't know," Longarm said as his hands tightened on the Winchester. He was thinking of that gang of outlaws Dewey Arquette had told him about. "But until we find out, we better stay out of sight."

Chapter 10

The sun was down and twilight had fallen over the landscape. Longarm knew that unless someone was actually looking for the wagon, it would be hard to spot where it was parked in the brush. He and Harriet were still several yards off the trail and as long as they stayed down, he thought there was a good chance the horsebackers would ride past without noticing them.

The riders were coming from the north, toward Fort Stockton. Longarm found himself wondering if Colonel Bascomb had sent out another patrol. Judging from the sound of the hoofbeats, a good-sized group was approaching; about the right size to be a cavalry patrol, in fact.

But as Longarm crouched in the brush next to Harriet, he took off his hat and raised his head enough to take a gander at the men riding past. They weren't cavalry troopers. He could tell that much by their headgear.

In the fading light, he saw all sorts of hats, from the flat-crowned Kansas style to the tall Montana pinch, from huge Mexican sombreros to derbies with tightly rolled brims. There were probably sixteen or seventeen men in the bunch, but they were all civilians. Longarm had no doubt about that.

What was a group like that doing out here? he asked himself. The answer that immediately suggested itself to his brain made him frown.

"Who do you think they were, Custis?" Harriet asked when the riders had swept on past and the only sign they left behind was a faint echo of hoofbeats and a thin haze of dust in the air above the road.

"Sheriff Arquette told me about a gang of outlaws that's been raising hell around these parts for the past year or so," Longarm said as he straightened from his crouch. "You heard anything about them?"

"Of course. There have been a lot of rumors about an organized gang. But no one has ever been able to catch them, or even prove that they exist." She caught hold of his arm. "Do you think it was that gang that just rode past?"

"Could've been," Longarm said. "But I reckon it could've been a crew from some ranch, heading back home after taking a trail herd up to the railroad in Fort Stockton. There's no way of knowing."

Her hand was still on his arm, and she stood close to him. He felt a shudder go through her. "I'm glad we got off the road when we did," she said. "I wouldn't have liked for them to catch us out there. If they were outlaws, I mean."

"Probably a good thing we made camp when we did, all right." He took a look around, saw that no one else seemed to be moving in the vast, shadow-haunted landscape, and continued, "Let's get on back. Uncle Dan ought to have supper ready before too much longer."

When they returned to the wagon, the old-timer did indeed have preparations for the meal well under way. He looked up from where he hunkered beside the fire and said, "I heard a bunch o' folks go past on horseback. Got any notion who they were?"

"We saw them," Harriet replied. "We couldn't tell for sure, but Marshal Long thinks they may be those outlaws we've heard about, the ones who have been robbing banks and holding up trains all over West Texas."

"You reckon?" Uncle Dan said, sounding excited. "And the two o' y'all seen 'em?"

"We didn't get a good look at them," Longarm explained. "We were about fifty yards off the trail when they rode past."

"How many were there?"

"Somewhere between fifteen and twenty. I couldn't say for sure."

Uncle Dan nodded. "A big enough bunch to raise plenty o' holy ned. I'm glad they didn't pay us a visit." He took the big frying pan off the fire. "Well, bacon's done. Grab your plates and come an' get it."

When they all had plates heaped with food and were sitting around the fire, Longarm asked the old-timer, "Did you ever drive a chuck wagon for a trail herd? The way you talk reminds me a little of a trail cook."

Uncle Dan chuckled. "You been up the trail, have you, son?"

"A time or two," Longarm said with a nod. "I rode for several Texas spreads and helped take herds to Kansas."

"Must've been a while ago."

"Not long after the war," Longarm admitted. "I wasn't much more than a kid."

"You take up arms in the great conflict?"

"I did. Just don't ask me on which side. I sort of disremember."

Uncle Dan laughed again. "I know what you're sayin'. I can't quite recall the color o' my uniform, neither." He took a healthy swallow of coffee. "But to answer your question, I did the cookin' on quite a few trail drives back in them days."

"I'm not surprised," Longarm said. "I thought I tasted a little peppermint in the Arbuckle's. That's the way our coosies always did it."

"Durned right. No point in ruinin' a cup o' perfectly good coffee with a bunch o' sugar an' cream."

Harriet laughed and said, "I have a feeling you two can sit here and talk about the old days all night long. I think I'm going to turn in and get some sleep, even though I'm sure the conversation would be quite interesting."

"You do that, gal," Uncle Dan told her. "Leave us two old fossils to reminisce."

Harriet glanced at Longarm. "I wouldn't say Marshal Long is all that old."

Uncle Dan snorted and said, "I'd bet his saddle's older than you."

Longarm just smiled and didn't say anything. There was some truth to what Uncle Dan said. He didn't think his saddle was actually as old as Harriet . . . but it damned near was.

Harriet smiled, bid them good night, and climbed up into the wagon. Longarm lit a cheroot while Uncle Dan packed tobacco into an old pipe and set it afire. He reached inside his vest and brought out a small silver flask.

"Now *this* is what that coffee really needs," he said quietly as he unscrewed the cap.

Longarm agreed and held out his cup so that Uncle Dan could add a dollop of whiskey from the flask to it. When he took a sip, he smacked his lips appreciatively and said, "Hits the spot."

"It damn sure does," the old-timer agreed. After a moment, he asked, "You really think them fellers you saw was owlhoots?"

"I think there's a good chance they were," Longarm said.

"It sounded like they was movin' right along."

"They were."

"That means they was headed somewhere in partic'lar, more than likely. What do you reckon they was goin' to do?"

Longarm had already asked himself that same question.

86

Now he shook his head and said, "I don't know. But I reckon it won't be anything good."

As a precaution, Longarm and Uncle Dan stood guard duty that night, trading off halfway through so that each of them could get some sleep. Longarm took the second turn, so he was awake when the stars paled and the eastern sky began to turn gray with the approach of dawn.

He had coffee boiling and biscuits baking when the other two woke up. "Say, I thought the cookin' was my job," Uncle Dan protested.

"I've ridden plenty of lonesome trails," Longarm said. "If I couldn't do a dab of cooking, I'd have starved to death 'fore now."

"I reckon you're right," the old-timer grumbled. "Bet a hat them biscuits ain't as light as mine, though."

"Were those biscuits we had last night?" Longarm asked with a grin. "I thought you'd slathered butter and molasses on some rocks."

"Rocks, is it? Rocks! Why, you young rapscallion, I'll have you know that when I was drivin' a chuck wagon, my biscuits was so light the punchers'd have to lasso 'em and pull 'em down outta the sky 'cause they kept tryin' to float off!"

"Here, try this," Longarm said, waving one of the biscuits he had just taken from the dutch oven up and down in his hand to cool it.

Uncle Dan took the biscuit and bit off a piece. As he chewed, he closed his eyes for a second in appreciation. Longarm saw that but didn't say anything about it.

"Passable," Uncle Dan said with a curt nod. "Passable, I reckon."

Harriet laughed and said to Longarm, "Here, give me one of those." She took a bite of the biscuit he handed her, and her eyes widened. "Oh. That is good." She glanced at her great-uncle. "No offense, Uncle Dan."

"Oh, I ain't offended. 'Tain't your fault you wasn't raised to know the diff'rence 'tween good cookin' and passable cookin'."

The good-natured squabbling continued through the meal and the preparations for getting on the trail again. The night had passed quietly and peacefully, and Longarm was grateful for that.

The thing about peace and quiet was that a fella never knew how long it was going to last.

He figured they would reach Marathon sometime in the early afternoon. Colonel Bascomb had already sent men to the little cattletown and water stop on the Texas & New Orleans Railroad to look for the missing patrol, and they hadn't had any luck. Longarm figured he and his two companions would push on toward the Big Bend. That had been the original destination of the patrol. Maybe they had circled around Marathon for some reason, he thought.

It might take weeks of riding all over West Texas before they found some lead to the vanished troopers. Longarm was prepared to do that, but he wasn't sure Harriet and her great-uncle were. But they could turn around and head back to Fort Stockton any time they wanted to, he told himself.

Later that morning they were approaching one of the isolated farms that dotted the area when Longarm heard a dog barking. It was a deep, full-throated bark, the kind that came from a fairly large animal. And it went on steadily, too, without any let-up.

"Hear that?" Uncle Dan asked from the wagon seat. "The varmint sounds a mite upset about somethin'."

"Yeah, he does," Longarm agreed. He looked toward the adobe *jacal* belonging to the farmer. The shack stood about a hundred yards off the trail. The barking came from over there. "I think I'll take a look and see what's got the old boy so spooked."

"I'll come with you," Harriet said. She started to turn her horse toward the side of the trail.

Longarm held up a hand to stop her. "It would probably be better if you stayed here with the wagon," he told her.

"But if there's trouble, you might need help."

"If I holler, you can come a-runnin'. Otherwise just stay here with Uncle Dan."

"Maybe that'd be best, gal," the old-timer put in with a frown. Longarm figured Uncle Dan thought the barking might mean the same thing he thought it did.

Harriet didn't like being left out, but she nodded and said reluctantly, "All right. Just be careful, Custis."

"I intend to."

He kneed the roan into a trot and pulled the Winchester from the saddle boot as he approached the *jacal*. He couldn't see the dog until he circled the adobe hut. Then he spotted the animal, a big tan-colored cur. The dog stood stiff-legged, looking toward the rear of the *jacal*.

As Longarm drew nearer, the dog turned and rushed at him, snarling and growling. The roan danced away skittishly as the dog snapped at its legs.

"Back off!" Longarm roared at the dog. Somewhat cowed, the animal sank onto his belly and worked his way backward, still growling. Longarm saw a bloody streak in the fur on the dog's left shoulder. He didn't seem to be badly wounded, though.

Longarm looked past the cur toward the hut and saw what he had been afraid that he would see. Two bodies lay there, not far from the rear wall of the *jacal*. A man and a woman, both middle-aged and dressed in the rough clothing of farmers. The man had been shot numerous times; his normally white shirt and pants were almost black with dried blood. His face had been obliterated. It looked like someone had emptied a six-gun into it at close range.

The woman lay on her back, her skirt around her hips

and her legs splayed open obscenely. She stared sightlessly up at the sky. A black-rimmed bullet hole was in the middle of her forehead, looking almost like a third eye. It appeared she had been shot only the one time.

They had raped her until they were tired of their vicious sport, Longarm thought, and then had put a bullet through her brain. Her husband had probably been dead already, although they might have forced him to watch and then killed him.

Either way they were bastards, and at that moment Longarm would have cheerfully strung them all up by their heels and lit fires under their heads.

With his face set in bleak lines, he drew a deep breath and then swung his horse around. As he rode back toward the waiting wagon, he glanced behind him and saw that the big tan dog was following him. The dog's master and mistress were dead and at least Longarm was human. Instinct made the dog trot after him.

Harriet and Uncle Dan knew something was wrong by the look on Longarm's face as he rode up. "There's been trouble here, ain't there?" the old-timer asked.

Longarm nodded as he reined in. "The man and woman who farmed this place are both dead, shot down behind the *jacal*." He didn't mention what had happened to the woman before she was killed. "Hand me the shovel from the wagon and I'll go get started on the burying."

"We can help you," Harriet offered.

"No, you stay here. If I need a hand, Uncle Dan can help."

Harriet looked like she wanted to argue again, but then she changed her mind and said, "It's worse than what you're telling us, isn't it?"

"It's bad enough," Longarm said grimly. "I reckon if there was any doubt about those fellas we saw last night being up to no good, it's gone now."

"You think they're responsible for this?"

Longarm pointed to a welter of hoofprints at the side of the trail. "They left the road here and then they came back and kept on going south. This was just a little side trip for them." His voice was tinged with bitter anger as he added that last comment.

"The folks who lived here wouldn't have had anything worth stealin'," Uncle Dan pointed out. "What happened was just out of sheer meanness."

Longarm nodded. "That's what it looks like to me, too." He took the shovel that the old man handed up to him. "Keep an eye out," he said as he wheeled his horse and rode back toward the adobe hut.

The dog sat down beside the wagon and looked up at Harriet and Uncle Dan. His bushy tail wagged, just a little.

By the time Longarm finished with his grim chore, it was past noon and he was soaked with sweat. When he rode back to the wagon, he saw Harriet trying to give a biscuit to the dog. The big cur growled and slunk backward as she approached. When she stopped and didn't come any closer, the dog quit growling and looked at her in mute appeal.

Harriet sighed in frustration. "You can tell he's hungry and I think he wants to be friends. Why won't he take the biscuit?"

"Because he doesn't trust you," Longarm said as he took off his hat and sleeved sweat from his forehead. "I don't reckon he trusts anybody right now. See that blood on his shoulder?"

"Yes, I could tell he'd been hurt."

"Probably shot and grazed by the same buzzards who killed those folks. They may have thought they'd killed him, too. He's lucky they didn't."

"Maybe we should call him Lucky."

Longarm frowned. "Why do we have to call him anything?"

Uncle Dan spoke up. "Because the gal's got it in her head that we got to take that mutt with us. Says we can't just leave him out here by hisself." He added ruefully, "She's soft-hearted like that."

Harriet ignored her great-uncle and bent over to place the biscuit on the ground. Then she backed well away from it. The dog looked at the biscuit, looked at the humans, and finally came forward hesitantly. He was obviously ready to flee if anybody tried to get close to him.

They stayed back until the dog had picked up the biscuit and gobbled it down. "Throw him another 'un," Uncle Dan suggested.

Harriet did so and the dog ate that biscuit, too.

"Well, you'll never get rid of him now," Uncle Dan said with a chuckle. "Once you've fed a dog, he'll tag along after you from then on."

"Tag," Harriet said. "That's an even better name."

Longarm and Uncle Dan looked at each other, grinned, and shook their heads.

When they headed for Marathon again a short time later, there were four of them, not three. Tag padded along behind the wagon, his bright red tongue lolling out as he followed his new companions.

Chapter 11

The delay at the farm meant that it was the middle of the afternoon before they neared Marathon. Longarm recalled hearing that the settlement had gotten its name from a retired sea captain who thought the countryside hereabouts looked like Greece. Never having been there, Longarm couldn't say whether that was right or not. To him it just looked like West Texas.

"Lot of smoke comin' up about where the town is," Uncle Dan pointed out when they were still a couple of miles from the settlement.

"Yeah, I noticed it a ways back," Longarm said. "Don't much care for the looks of it, either."

Harriet asked, "Do you think those outlaws raided the town?"

"Could be. We'll know soon enough," Longarm said.

They moved on and soon came within sight of the settlement itself. Just as Longarm feared, the black column of smoke climbing into the blue sky came from one of the buildings. He spurred ahead to find out what had happened. Harriet was right behind him and Tag yapped along at her horse's heels.

The inside of the building was burned out already, and

the roof had collapsed, as had a couple of the walls. The walls that still stood were burning now. The street was crowded with people. They had formed a line from the public well and were passing buckets of water from hand to hand so that the buildings on either side of the burning structure could be saved. The bucket brigade soaked the walls and threw water on the roofs of those buildings.

Not everyone was engaged in passing the buckets. Longarm brought the roan to a stop and asked a couple of bystanders, "What happened here?"

"Outlaws," one of the men replied. He pointed to the burning building. "That was our bank, damn it! After they'd cleaned it out, they threw a couple of sticks of dynamite inside and blew the hell out of it!"

The other man said, "That set the place on fire and there was nothing we could do. It went up too fast to stop it."

"But they robbed the bank first, you said?"

"Pistol-whipped old Clarence Wilson, the bank manager," the first man said bitterly. "And then the bastards left him in there when they blew it up!" He glanced at Harriet. "Pardon my language, ma'am."

"No need to apologize," she told him. "Those men obviously *are* bastards."

"Got any law hereabouts?" Longarm asked.

"The county sheriff over at Alpine," the man replied. "And we've got a town marshal."

"Where is he?"

The man turned and pointed to a shape in the street that was covered by a piece of canvas. Longarm saw dark splotches on the canvas that could only be blood.

"Right there," the citizen said. "He ran out with a scattergun and tried to stop those owlhoots, but they gunned him down."

"He never had a chance," the second man said. "There were more than a dozen of those outlaws."

"Anybody get a good look at them, maybe recognized some of them?"

The first man shook his head. "They were all masked. Say, mister, what business is it of yours, anyway?"

"I'm a lawman," Longarm replied without hesitation. On a lot of his cases, he concealed his true identity and worked undercover, but on this job, it didn't really matter. "Deputy U.S. marshal."

That caught the attention of several other townspeople. One of them called out, "Hey, Marshal, are you goin' after those bank robbers?" The crowd looked at him expectantly, awaiting his answer.

So were Harriet and Uncle Dan. They knew the real reason he had come to Marathon was to look for the missing cavalry patrol. But Longarm still couldn't shake his hunch that the answer to the patrol's disappearance might lie with the gang of outlaws.

"I'll see what I can do," he said. Ever since he had seen what the outlaws had done to that Mexican farmer and his wife, Longarm had been looking for an excuse to go after the gang. This raid on Marathon had given him that excuse.

A stocky man in a suit came bustling up to him. "Did I hear you say you're a lawman?"

"That's right." Longarm swung down from the saddle and faced the man. "Deputy U.S. Marshal Custis Long."

"I'm Josiah Hargrove, the mayor of Marathon. I speak for the whole town when I say we'll give you any help we can, Marshal. Those bastards killed at least four people, maybe more. We won't know for sure until we go through what's left of the bank."

"Which way did they go when they rode out?"

Hargrove turned and pointed. "They headed south, riding hellbent-for-leather."

That would take them straight toward the Big Bend, thought Longarm. That was the most rugged, isolated, and

sparsely populated part of Texas. There were a few settlements down there, such as Lajitas and Presidio, but mostly
it was just empty deserts and mountains. Until a few years
earlier, the Comanches had held sway over the region, and
their famous War Trail that led in and out of Mexico was
still easily seen. The army had finally succeeded in running
out the Comanches, but from time to time Apaches still
raided from below the border.

Longarm glanced at Harriet. He didn't like the idea of
taking a woman down into that hell country. He had a feeling she wouldn't cotton to being left behind, though. Not
only had the outlaws fled in that direction, but the Big Bend
might also hold the answer to the riddle of what had happened to the missing cavalry troopers.

"Are you going after them, Marshal?" Mayor Hargrove
asked.

Longarm nodded slowly. "I reckon I am. Not today,
though. We need to stock up on supplies and our horses
could use some rest. It'll be dark in a few hours, too. We
couldn't get very far before we'd have to stop."

Hargrove frowned. "They've only got a two-hour lead.
If you wait until morning, that'll be more like fourteen or
fifteen hours."

The mayor was right and Longarm knew it, but that
didn't change things. He might be able to trail the outlaws
after dark, but that would be risky and he could wind up
losing the trail entirely. It would be better to wait until
morning and get a fresh start . . . and maybe by then he
could talk Harriet into either going back to Fort Stockton
or staying here in Marathon.

"I'll find 'em," he told Hargrove. "Don't worry about
that. A bunch that big is going to have a hard time hiding,
even in the Big Bend."

But that cavalry patrol, which was about the same size
as the gang, had dropped out of sight, and no one had been

able to find them. The thought was an unpleasant reminder of the task he had facing him.

Marathon had one hotel, an adobe building with a yellow-painted façade. Longarm got rooms there for himself, Harriet, and Uncle Dan, even though the old-timer grumbled about the expense and insisted he could sleep under the wagon just fine.

"This is liable to be the last time any of us sleep in a real bed for a long time," Longarm told him. "Might as well enjoy it."

He spent the rest of the afternoon loading up on supplies, packing as much food and ammunition into the back of the wagon as he could. He made sure all the water barrels and canteens were filled, too. And he talked to the townspeople, asking them about the bank robbers, trying to find out as much as possible about the desperadoes responsible for the raid. The descriptions he was given tallied with what he and Harriet had seen from the brush the night before.

That had been a mighty near thing, Longarm thought. If the gang had stumbled over them, they would have put up a fight, of course, but the odds against them almost guaranteed that by now he and Harriet and Uncle Dan would be dead.

Longarm did learn one other thing from his conversations with the townspeople: they were in general agreement that the leader of the gang was a big, bald man who wore a derby hat and sported bright red suspenders attached to his trousers. It would be hard to miss an hombre who looked like that if they ran across him, Longarm thought.

He also paid a visit to the tiny telegraph office adjacent to the equally small railroad station and sent a wire to Dewey Arquette, letting him know what had happened in

Marathon, even though the towns were in different counties and officially Marathon was out of Dewey's bailiwick. Mayor Hargrove had already notified the sheriff of Alpine in Brewster County about the outrage.

That evening, Longarm, Harriet, and Uncle Dan had supper in the hotel's dining room. A waitress in a long skirt and an embroidered peasant blouse brought them platters of enchiladas, tamales, frijoles, chiles, and tortillas. The food was good, especially when it was washed down with mugs of beer. Harriet, more ladylike, settled for lemonade.

After they had eaten, Longarm walked down to the livery stable to check on their horses. The dog that Harriet had named Tag was sitting just outside the barn, almost like he was on guard duty.

The hostler, a heavyset Mexican who had introduced himself earlier as Javier Gonzales, gestured toward Tag and said, "He sits there like that and won't let nobody come near him. When nobody bothers him, though, he looks like he wants to be friends. He is just scared, no?"

"He lost the folks who owned him and got shot, to boot," Longarm said. "I reckon it'll be a while before he trusts anybody again." He took out a tortilla that he had rolled up and stuck in his pocket during supper. "Here you go, old son," he said as he tossed the tortilla in Tag's direction.

The dog stood up slowly and advanced cautiously on the tortilla. He sniffed it for a moment, then picked it up in his mouth and ate it.

"I got some scraps I can give him," Gonzales offered.

"I'd be much obliged," Longarm said as he took out a cheroot. He snapped a lucifer into life with his thumbnail and lit the tightly rolled cylinder of tobacco. He drew the smoke into his lungs as he strolled back toward the hotel.

He met Harriet on the way. She had a paper-wrapped bundle in her hands. "I was able to get some kitchen scraps for Tag," she explained as she lifted the bundle.

Despite the overall grimness of the day's developments, Longarm chuckled. "You ain't the only one who had that idea. I got a feeling that dog's liable to wind up being mighty well-fed."

He walked with Harriet to the livery stable, where Tag ate the scraps, but only after Harriet had set them down and backed away. Then they returned together to the hotel.

"I'll be starting pretty early in the morning," Longarm told her as they paused outside the door of her room. "I want to be on the trail as soon as it's light enough to see the tracks those owlhoots left."

"I'll be ready," Harriet promised.

"I've been wanting to talk to you about that," Longarm began.

She held up a hand to stop him. "Don't even start trying to convince me not to go with you, Custis."

"Dadgum it, I'm trying to track down a bunch of outlaws!" he said. "They're nothing but snake-blooded killers, Harriet. You've seen that for yourself."

"They might know what happened to Scott and the rest of that patrol. As long as that chance exists, I have to come along."

The time had come for some honesty, no matter how brutal it might be, Longarm decided. He said, "There's a good chance Lieutenant Morgan and the rest of those troopers are dead."

She took a sharply indrawn breath and her chin lifted. "I know that. The outlaws may have ambushed them and killed them."

"And if that turns out to be the case, you reckon you can avenge them all by yourself?"

"Of course not." She smiled faintly. "That's why I've got you and Uncle Dan along."

Longarm was ready to argue some more, but again she stopped him. "Remember what you said about not sending us back to Fort Stockton?"

"You mean about how you'd be liable to follow me anyway, even if you said you were going back?"

She nodded. "That's right. And it's still true. Unless you take us back to Fort Stockton yourself, you can't be sure that we're not still right behind you, Custis. I don't think you want that."

"No, I don't," he admitted. "But what I was thinking was that you might stay here and your uncle could go with me. He seems like a right salty old cuss."

"So you'd take him and abandon me?" she snapped.

"I just don't want anything to happen to you, Harriet."

"I appreciate that. But I can ride and handle a gun. I can take care of myself. I won't hold you back or be a burden, Custis." Her voice had taken on a hard edge of anger.

"I never said that you would."

"But that's what you're thinking," she insisted. She crossed her arms over her breasts and glared at him stubbornly.

"All right," he said after a moment. "I give up. I ain't in the habit of surrendering, though, and I don't much like it. I may not be very good company."

"I'm not interested in company. I just want to find out what happened to that missing patrol."

"So do I," Longarm said. "And there may come a time when you have to do some of that riding and shooting you were talking about. There won't be anybody down there in the Big Bend to give us a hand if we run into trouble."

"That's all right with me. We'll be just fine."

Longarm hoped she was right . . . and hoped that he wasn't making one of the worst mistakes of his long career.

Chapter 12

There was a telegram from Dewey Arquette waiting for Longarm in the morning. "I didn't think I ought to wake you when the boy brought it over late last night, Marshal," the clerk at the hotel explained as he handed Longarm the yellow telegraph flimsy with a crudely printed message lettered on it in pencil. "You weren't leaving until this morning anyway."

Longarm suppressed the irritation he felt. He didn't like anybody else making such decisions for him. There was no point in bitching at the clerk, though, since he would soon be leaving Marathon.

He scanned the message from Dewey and nodded to himself. According to this, Dewey had gotten word that a few days earlier a gang of robbers had held up the bank in Ozona, one county to the east of Fort Stockton.

The timing worked out right. The gang that had hit Marathon could be the same one. There was something a little odd about that, however. According to what Dewey had told him when they first talked about it, the gang never pulled two jobs that close together. Their crimes had been spread out over a number of months.

Maybe they were just getting greedy, Longarm told himself. He read the rest of the message.

When he had wired the young lawman in Fort Stockton the day before, Longarm had given him the descriptions of the outlaws he had gotten from the townspeople. Other than the big bald man in the derby who had seemed to be the leader, those descriptions were pretty sketchy.

But none of the reports of previous hold-ups included any mention of the bald man, Dewey's telegram said. That didn't jibe, either, Longarm thought with a frown. Something was mighty odd about this.

He would ponder on it and try to figure it out later, he told himself. For now, he and Harriet and Uncle Dan needed to get on the trail. The street outside was already gray with approaching dawn.

He knocked on the doors of their rooms to rouse them and then went into the hotel dining room where a sleepy waitress poured coffee for him and took his order back to the kitchen. He ordered for his two companions as well, so their food was already on the table when they entered the dining room a short time later.

"I don't reckon you've changed your mind about going along?" Longarm said to Harriet.

Before Harriet could reply, Uncle Dan snorted and said, "This gal change her mind about anything once she's made it up? That ain't likely to happen in our lifetime, son."

"I'm going," she said curtly.

Longarm looked over at the old-timer. "She tells me she's a good shot."

"Oh, she is. I told you that, too."

"Even without her spectacles?" Longarm turned his gaze to Harriet. "You ain't had them since you left Fort Stockton. I know, because I've got 'em."

She had the good grace to flush slightly in embarrassment. "You found them? I wondered what happened to them. But as I'm sure you know by now, I don't really need them. I can see fine without them."

"Why wear them, then?" Longarm wanted to know.

"I'm sure this has never occurred to you," she said somewhat acidly, "but most women have a hard time getting men to take them seriously. They see an attractive face and never stop to think that there might be a brain behind it."

Longarm shrugged. "Some fellas are that way, I reckon. Not all of them, though."

"Enough so that I've found it's easier to do my work if I wear the spectacles. That way the men I deal with don't think I'm just some flighty girl who doesn't really know how to do anything."

What she was saying made some sense to Longarm. He said, "I've got them wrapped up nice and snug in one of my saddlebags if you want 'em back."

"No, that's all right. Maybe it's time I stopped depending on them." Her chin lifted defiantly. "If the men I run into are too blasted stubborn to accept me the way I am, it's their loss."

"Sounds right to me," Longarm agreed.

They finished their breakfast, paid for it, and went outside. Javier Gonzales and his helpers at the livery stable had saddled the horses, hitched up the team, and brought mounts and wagon down to the hotel, just as Longarm had arranged for the night before.

The dog was waiting beside the wagon. His tail swished back and forth in the dust of the street as Longarm, Harriet, and Uncle Dan approached. Before they got there, though, Tag stood up and backed off. At least this morning he didn't growl, just regarded the humans warily.

Harriet had brought leftovers from her breakfast for him. She put them on the ground and stepped away. Tag came forward to eat without hesitating quite so long this time.

Longarm and Uncle Dan checked over the wagon and

the animals and found that Gonzales had done a good job getting everything ready. They fetched what little gear was in their rooms in the hotel, loaded it in the wagon, and then were ready to leave Marathon.

As Longarm and Harriet rode past the still-smoldering ruins that were all that was left of the bank and Uncle Dan trundled the wagon along behind them, they saw that men were already at work clearing away the debris. Mayor Hargrove stepped out from the crew to meet them.

"You're ready to take up the trail?" he asked.

Longarm nodded. "Yep, we're on our way after the skunks who did this."

"We found three bodies inside the bank," Hargrove said grimly. "The manager, a teller, and a customer, as far as we can tell. And those outlaws shot down two people in the street as they rode out, including our marshal. So that's five murders on top of the robbery."

"They've got a lot to answer for," Longarm agreed.

Hargrove looked at Harriet. "Miss, you're going along?" He sounded like he didn't think it was a good idea.

"That's right," Harriet said shortly, as if daring the mayor to argue with her.

Hargrove just shrugged. "Good luck to you." He looked at Longarm again. "Good luck to all of you." He added heavily, "You're liable to need it."

Longarm sure couldn't argue with that.

The road that led from Marathon down into the Big Bend country wasn't heavily traveled, so Longarm had no trouble picking up the tracks of the gang. The outlaws didn't seem to be going to any trouble to conceal their trail.

Longarm suspected that sooner or later that would change. They hadn't expected any pursuit from Marathon after blowing up the bank and setting the place on fire; they had known that the townspeople would all be occupied with keeping the fire from spreading.

But if they had a hide-out down in the Big Bend, they wouldn't want the army or the Texas Rangers—or even a federal marshal playing a mostly lone hand—to find it easily. It would take all of Longarm's skill as a tracker to locate the hide-out.

Heat built in the air as the sun rose higher. The sky today was a cloudless pale blue, without even a hint of clouds. By afternoon the sun would be a fierce, brassy red ball and the sky would turn a flat, pallid silver color that hurt the eye to look at for too long. When that happened, the travelers might have to find some shade somewhere and wait out the worst of the heat.

They could still push on for a long time before it got that bad, though.

Around the middle of the day, Harriet said, "I swear, I don't think those mountains are a bit closer, even though it seems like they're only a few miles away."

"That's the way it'll seem until we get to 'em, too," Longarm said. "Those are the Santiagos. Beyond them you've got the Chalk Mountains, then along the river itself are the Chisos and the Chinatis."

Harriet looked over at him. "You sound like you're pretty familiar with the area."

"I've been down here a time or two. Last time I wound up falling into Santa Elena Canyon."

She lifted her eyebrows. "You fell in a canyon?"

"Yep. Pretty deep one, too."

"But you survived the fall."

Longarm grinned. "I'm here, ain't I? That was the same job where I got dragged into a little dust-up on the other side of the border. Nearly had to make an old extinct volcano erupt to settle that one."

"A volcano," Harriet repeated.

"Sure enough," Longarm said solemnly.

"It sounds as though you've led an . . . eventful . . . life, Custis."

"I reckon I've had my share of excitement," he admitted. "Maybe more than my share."

They rode on, stopping only for a quick lunch and a brief rest for the horses. During the morning, Longarm had kept an eye out for any sign that the outlaws had made camp the night before, but he hadn't seen any. He had worried about the possibility they wouldn't stop but would just ride on through the night, thereby increasing their lead. But there hadn't been anything he could do about it.

While they were stopped, he brought out a pair of field glasses from his saddle bags and checked their back trail, being careful to shade the lenses with one hand so the sun wouldn't reflect off them and warn anyone who might be following them.

However, he didn't see anyone back there. That did a little to ease his mind, but he didn't relax completely. The man who had bushwhacked him on the way to Marathon had been *ahead* of him, not behind.

"What are you looking for?" Harriet asked.

Longarm explained.

"I'm still not sure I understand that," Harriet said. "Who could be sending hired killers after you?"

"There are plenty of people around who have grudges against me." Longarm paused and then added, "For a while there, I wondered if you had anything to do with it."

She looked sharply at him and said, "What?"

"Well, think about it," he went on. They were out in front of the wagon by twenty yards or so and when he lowered his voice Uncle Dan wouldn't be able to hear him. "You made arrangements to meet me in my room at the Pecos House and said you'd be there later. You knew I was going to stop and pick up a bottle of whiskey on the way. That gave you enough time so that you could've met those killers and told 'em where to find me."

"I can't believe you were suspicious of *me*, Custis. After what happened between us . . ."

"No offense," he said, "but it wouldn't have been the first time some gal who wanted me dead tried to use her feminine wiles on me. A fella in my line of work has to be suspicious of darned near everybody."

"I suppose so," she said grudgingly. "Still . . ." She shook her head. "I hope you at least trust me now."

"I reckon I do," Longarm said.

But to tell the truth, he still harbored a few small doubts. Harriet and Uncle Dan had done nothing but help him since he'd met up with them on the trail between Fort Stockton and Marathon. But some folks would say that they had come along mighty convenient-like, right after that fella had tried to bushwhack him.

Of course, if they really wanted him dead, they'd had plenty of chances to make another try for him since then. But maybe they had decided to string him along instead, staying close to him until they were ready to make their move. The whole thing was unlikely, sure enough, but Longarm couldn't rule it out completely.

Harriet *did* have a history of deception, after all. She hadn't told him that she was romantically involved with the missing Lieutenant Morgan until he had forced it out of her and she had worn those fake spectacles to help her pretend to be something she really wasn't.

What else was she pretending about?

Longarm couldn't answer that question. All he could do was play along and wait to see what happened.

They stopped in the middle of the afternoon, stretching out in the meager shade of some mesquites to doze and wait for the worst of the heat to be over. One of them stayed awake at all times, on guard for possible trouble. Once the sun had lowered enough in the western sky so that the air wasn't quite as searingly hot, they started south again, following the tracks left by the band of outlaws.

Longarm knew they hadn't closed the gap much, if any, on the owlhoots. But they weren't any farther back, either, and the trail was still relatively easy to follow. The ground was getting harder and rockier, though. It might not be long before they would reach a stretch of stony ground that wouldn't take hoofprints very well, if at all. Then the pursuit would get really challenging.

"Cold camp tonight," Longarm announced late in the afternoon. "A fire is visible for a long way out here. No point in telling those old boys we're behind them."

"Makes sense to me," Uncle Dan said. "That's why I cooked extra beans and biscuits at lunch." He sighed. "I will miss my coffee, though."

So would Longarm, but they would just have to make do without it for a while.

They camped beside a huge boulder that thrust up beside the trail. Longarm checked the area good for snakes. The varmints would den up anywhere there was shade during the day. He didn't find any rattlers, so he nodded his approval and motioned for Uncle Dan to park the wagon there.

They staked out the horses on a patch of mostly dry grass. They had brought grain from Marathon to use as feed, but it made sense to let the animals graze as much as they could.

After the cold supper, Harriet climbed into the wagon to sleep. Longarm spread a lariat in a wide circle around the vehicle. The rough rope would keep any night-roaming serpents from crawling over it and invading the men's bedrolls. Longarm knew more than one man who had gotten careless and wound up with a diamondback rattler for a bedmate. That could make for a mighty unpleasant awakening.

He stood the first watch, sitting with his back propped against one of the wagon wheels while Uncle Dan crawled under the wagon and went to sleep. Longarm laid his Winchester across his lap and listened to the small sounds of the night. Somewhere off in the distance, a coyote howled and a few minutes later several more joined the chorus. It was a lonesome song, but it had a certain melancholy sweetness about it. Of course, after a while Uncle Dan's snoring drowned it out . . .

That was when the wagon shifted slightly on its springs and Harriet climbed out.

Chapter 13

Longarm came smoothly to his feet as Harriet stepped down to the ground from the tailgate. He was alert and ready for trouble.

"What's wrong?" he hissed, keeping his voice low so he wouldn't disturb Uncle Dan unless it was necessary. A few feet away, Tag sat up, twitching his ears forward.

"Nothing's wrong," Harriet whispered, "except that I can't sleep."

Longarm felt a flash of irritation. He had the frontiersman's knack of being able to fall asleep almost instantly, whenever and wherever he had the chance. Only when he was turning over a particularly thorny puzzle in his mind did he have trouble dozing off. He didn't have much patience with people who had trouble sleeping.

But he pushed that feeling away. Harriet wasn't him and he couldn't hold her to his standards. He said, "Something bothering you?"

"Yes, very much." She hesitated for a second and then said, "Let's go around on the other side of the rock and talk about it. Do you mind, Custis?"

Longarm frowned in the darkness. He didn't much like leaving the wagon unguarded . . . but Tag was there, and

Longarm was confident the big cur would pitch a fit if anybody tried to sneak up on them. And Uncle Dan slept with a scattergun and a Winchester beside him, close at hand in case of trouble.

"All right," he said with a curt nod. "But we won't go very far."

"No, just around on the other side of the rock."

What the hell was she up to? Why was she so insistent that they put the big rock between themselves and the wagon?

Was this another trap?

Longarm didn't think so, but he kept his hands wrapped tightly around the Winchester as he and Harriet walked quietly around the rock. When they were on the far side of it, with its tons of upthrust mass between them and the wagon, she stopped and turned to him.

"Custis . . ." she whispered.

Then her body was pressed against his, all the sweet warm curves of it molded to his hard, muscular frame, and her lips found his in a hot, searching kiss.

Longarm had the rifle in his right hand. He didn't put it down. But he put his left on her back and caressed her. Her arms went around his neck. Her tongue slid out. He opened his mouth and met her tongue with his.

For a long moment the sensuous duel continued. Harriet slipped a hand between them and cupped his stiffening manhood through his trousers. She still had hold of it when she pulled her head back and whispered, "Please don't think I'm a . . . a terrible woman, Custis."

"Never entered my mind," Longarm said. It was only a half-truth. He didn't think she was terrible because of what she was doing now, but he still hadn't forgotten about that ambush in the Pecos House . . .

"I couldn't sleep because I kept thinking about you and about what we did back in Fort Stockton. I know I said it

112

would never happen again, but . . . I don't think I can honor that promise."

"You got to do what you think is right," Longarm told her.

She moaned softly as she caressed his shaft. "I can't think of anything that's more right than this."

At least he understood now why she had wanted to come around here. They couldn't very well have climbed in the wagon and romped there only a couple of feet above Uncle Dan's head. As it was, they could still hear his snores from the other side of the rock, but if he woke up he wouldn't be able to see what they were doing.

She stepped back. The dress she wore buttoned down the front, unlike the one she'd had on that night in Fort Stockton. Her fingers fairly flew as she undid the buttons. As she spread it open, Longarm saw that she had taken off everything underneath it. She dropped the dress to the ground and stood there totally nude.

She was beautiful in the silvery moonlight, all pale, graceful curves and dark, intriguing hollows. She moved into his arms again, even though he was still fully dressed, and whispered, "Touch me, Custis. Touch me all over."

He did as she asked, stroking and caressing her as he leaned down and kissed her lips, her nose, and her forehead. He cupped her breasts and thumbed her nipples, then slid his hands over her flanks and around her hips, filling his hands with her buttocks. He squeezed and lifted them, parting the cheeks and slipping a finger into the dark valley between them to tease the tight opening there. Harriet leaned her head against his shoulder and gasped with desire and excitement as he intimately explored her. He reached between her legs with his other hand and she parted her thighs so that he could caress the folds of her sex. She was already drenched with womanly juices.

She trembled as he worked a finger in and out of her and after only a moment she clutched at him and cried out softly as a climax shook her. Longarm held her until the spasms subsided.

"Your turn," she said breathlessly.

She sank to her knees in front of him and went to work. In moments she had his trousers and long underwear down and was fisting his huge erection. She grasped the shaft in both hands and rubbed the head of it all over her face. Her tongue darted out and teased the opening, licking up the pearl of moisture that had seeped from it. She cupped the heavy sacs as she continued licking up and down the length of the thick pole of heated male flesh.

Finally she took the head in her mouth and sucked on it. That sent such sweet sensations cascading through Longarm that he almost spent then and there.

She stopped what she was doing just before she sent him over the edge and when she stood up she whispered urgently, "I need you in me, Custis."

Longarm turned so that his back was pressed against the rock. He still wore his shirt, so his skin was protected from the rough surface. The rock was still pleasantly warm from the sun it had soaked up during the day.

As Harriet put her arms around his neck again, he reached around her, cupped her buttocks once more, and lifted her. She wrapped her legs around his hips. The tip of his shaft touched her wet, heated opening. She leaned back a little in his arms, adjusting the angle of their hips, and then slid down onto his manhood. Her arms tightened around his neck as he fully penetrated her.

Their hips worked together in perfect conjunction, rocking back and forth as his member pumped in and out of her. It was a damned good thing he had that big rock to brace himself against, he thought. Their movements became quicker as the excitement mounted in them. Longarm was gripped by urgency and he could tell that Harriet felt the same thing. He didn't try to hold back. Neither did she.

When he felt another climax rippling through her, he

thrust into her as deeply as he could and let go with his own, loosing spurt after white-hot spurt of seed into her. He emptied himself in a long series of explosions that filled her. Both of them were soaked from the mingling of their juices.

As the last shuddering spasms trailed away, Harriet lowered her head and rested it on his shoulder. Her breasts were flattened against him and he felt her heart beating heavily against his own.

Longarm leaned back against the big rock and held her like that for several minutes, until both of them were breathing relatively normally again. Then Harriet laughed softly and said, "You can put me down now."

"I ain't all that sure I want to," Longarm said.

She laughed again and wiggled her hips a little, making his still semi-erect organ shift deliciously inside her. "Yes, it's wonderful," she agreed, "but you can't stand there like that and hold me up all night."

"Be sort of nice to try," Longarm said with a grin. But he carefully disengaged himself from her and lowered her to the ground.

From the far side of the rock, Uncle Dan snorted in his sleep and then stopped snoring. Longarm tensed slightly. The old-timer had probably just turned over. The cessation of his snoring didn't have to mean anything.

But then a second later he heard Tag growl.

Longarm grabbed his trousers and underwear and pulled them up, then snatched the Winchester from where he had leaned it against the rock. He heard the sharp hiss as Harriet took a breath before saying something, and his hand shot out to close over her mouth. She started to struggle, but he put his mouth next to her ear and breathed, "Somebody may be skulking around the camp. Get dressed and stay here."

She nodded against his hand, signifying that she understood. He took his hand away and wrapped it around the

115

breech of the rifle instead. Moving slowly and carefully so that his boots wouldn't grate against the sand and gravel underfoot, he started around the rock toward the wagon.

Tag was still growling. Suddenly, the dog snarled loudly and then barked. A man's voice snapped, "Shoot that damned mutt!"

Longarm went around the rock in a rush and threw himself flat on the ground as he came in sight of the wagon. There was enough light from the moon and stars for him to be able to see two men standing beside the vehicle. Moonlight winked on the guns in their hands. Both of the intruders were taller than Uncle Dan and one wore a high-crowned Mexican sombrero. Longarm knew they were up to no good, so he opened fire as soon as he hit the ground.

The Winchester roared as flame gouted from its muzzle. The man in the sombrero was smashed back against the wagon by the lead. Longarm twisted onto his left side, propped on his elbow, as he worked the lever of the rifle to jack another round into the chamber. He fired again even as Colt flame bloomed in the darkness next to the wagon. A bullet smacked into the ground beside him. He didn't know if he had hit the second gunman or not.

The man let out a howl as Tag attacked him, sinking fangs into his leg. Hopping to one side as he tried to loosen the dog's grip, the man swung his Colt toward Tag.

Longarm leaped up from the ground and lunged forward, striking down with the barrel of the Winchester. It cracked across the wrist of the would-be killer's gun hand. The man cried out in pain again as he let go of the gun.

Longarm reversed the rifle and slammed the butt stock into the man's face. The man's head jerked back under the force of the blow. He crumpled, his legs folding up underneath him. Like a flash, Tag went for his throat.

Longarm thrust the rifle barrel between the dog and the man and held Tag back. It wasn't easy. The big cur probably weighed close to a hundred pounds and he was strong as an ox. Longarm finally looped an arm around the thickly-furred neck and dragged the dog away.

He was determined to take one of these men alive so that he could be questioned. Longarm got Tag well away from the man he had knocked out, then looked for the man in the sombrero.

He was gone.

Longarm's brain barely had time to register that fact when someone hit him from behind, spilling him to the ground. The fall jolted the Winchester out of his hands. He rolled over, trying to throw off the attacker. The man loomed over him, mostly in shadow, but Longarm could tell that he wore a charro jacket. Had to be the Mexican. A dark streak across his face was probably blood from where Longarm's hastily fired first shot had creased him.

The man fought with a furious frenzy. Longarm saw the glint of moonlight on a knife blade as his opponent jerked an arm up over his head. The imminent threat galvanized Longarm into action. He arched his back and heaved, sending the Mexican sprawling. Longarm rolled the other direction and came up on his hands and knees.

The enemy was even quicker. He was already up and his booted foot shot toward Longarm's face in a vicious kick. Longarm twisted aside, letting the brutal blow glance off his shoulder. There was still enough power behind it to stun him and knock him flat on his back.

With an incoherent shout of rage, the Mexican launched himself at Longarm with the knife poised to strike down into the big lawman's body. Before the killing stroke could fall, a six-gun blasted somewhere nearby, a pair of shots triggered quickly. Lead lashed into the man's body and twisted him in mid-air. He crashed to the ground beside Longarm. The knife went spinning away harmlessly.

Longarm turned his head to look above and behind him. He saw Harriet standing there, a smoking gun held leveled in front of her, in both hands. She said, "Is that all of them?"

She sounded surprisingly calm considering that she had just shot a man, Longarm thought as he scrambled to his feet. "I only saw two of them," he said as he picked up the Winchester. Holding the rifle ready just in case, he stepped over to the man Harriet had shot and rolled him onto his back with the toe of his boot. The way the man's arms and legs flopped loosely told Longarm that he was dead.

Longarm turned toward the other one. Tag sat a few yards from the man, watching him closely.

"I'll take care of this one," Longarm said. "Better check on Uncle Dan."

"Oh, my God," Harriet said as she lowered the gun. "You think they might have—"

She didn't waste any more time on talk but rushed over to the wagon instead. A dark, silent, motionless shape lay under it.

"Uncle Dan!" Harried cried anxiously as she crawled under the wagon to see if he was still alive.

Longarm went over to the first man and knelt beside him. The hombre wasn't moving at all. Longarm jabbed the muzzle of the Winchester against his shoulder and got no response. Muttering, the big lawman checked for a pulse in the killer's throat and then spat, "Damn!"

"He's alive!" Harriet called from under the wagon. "Uncle Dan is alive! I think they must have pistol-whipped him in his sleep, but he's breathing!"

"That's more than I can say for this one," Longarm responded bitterly. "Son of a bitch is dead as he can be."

And once more, the question of who was sending men after him to try to kill him would have to go unanswered.

Chapter 14

But at least he could be fairly certain now that Harriet and Uncle Dan weren't responsible for the attempts on his life, Longarm thought later as he sat with the two of them beside the wagon. Uncle Dan had a bandage tied around his grizzled head and he was complaining that all the imps of Hell had taken up residence inside his skull.

The old-timer had been attacked by the intruders and Harriet had done for one of them herself, quite possibly saving Longarm's life in the process. It no longer made sense to think that either of them could have sent the bushwhackers after Longarm.

"I woke up just enough to hear that dog whine," Uncle Dan was explaining. "Then something walloped me and I don't know nothin' after that."

"One of those varmints hit you with his gun, I reckon," Longarm said. "No way of knowing which one. They would have come looking for Harriet and me next, if Tag hadn't started growling and barking."

"Where was you two?" Uncle Dan asked as he rubbed his head. "No offense, Marshal, but I thought you was supposed to be guardin' the wagon."

"It was my fault," Harriet said quickly. "I thought I heard something around on the other side of the rock and I asked Custis to go check on it."

"Find anything?"

"Nope," Longarm said.

"Maybe them two varmints left their hosses around there somewhere."

"We'll find out in the morning. I reckon the horses have to be pretty close by."

"Shame about 'em both bein' dead." The old-timer grunted. "I would've liked to ask 'em a few questions. I knew an old Apache once who taught me a few things about gettin' folks to talk."

"I tried to get one of them alive," Longarm said, still feeling a little disgusted with himself. "But when I hit that fella in the face, I reckon I busted his nose so that the bone splinters went right up into his brain. He must've been dead even while I was dragging ol' Tag off of him."

Harriet reached out and ruffled the hair on top of the dog's head. He didn't pull away or even growl this time. It was as if now that he had fought side by side with these humans, he had fully accepted them.

"He's a good boy," Harriet said. "We make a pretty good team."

"You weren't lying about being able to use a gun," Longarm told her. "That was mighty fine shooting, the way you hit that old boy on the wing, so to speak. Saved my bacon, that's for sure. I *did* tell you to stay around on the other side of that rock, though."

She laughed. "Aren't you glad that I'm not very good at taking orders?"

"I reckon in this case I am," Longarm allowed. "Next time, though, it might be a good idea to listen to me."

Uncle Dan asked, "You reckon there's gonna be a next time?"

"Somebody seems bound and determined to see me

dead," Longarm said grimly. "I figure we can count on there being a next time."

He had dragged both bodies around on the other side of the rock after searching them. He hadn't found anything in their pockets except a considerable amount of money—two hundred dollars each.

Two hundred dollars American, Longarm thought . . . The price of a life. Or in this case, three lives, since he had no doubt the two gunmen would have killed Harriet and Uncle Dan, too.

Harriet insisted that her great-uncle climb into the wagon and sleep in the built-in bunk. "You've been injured; you need the rest," she said. "I'll be fine under the wagon and I'll spell Custis on guard duty after a while."

"You're sure?" the old-timer said.

"Certain. Go on now. Get some sleep."

Muttering about how he was going to go soft with treatment like this, Uncle Dan climbed in the wagon. Harriet stretched out on top of the blankets spread out underneath the vehicle.

"Wake me when you get tired," she told Longarm. "And don't worry about trusting me to stand guard. I can handle the job."

Longarm nodded. After what he had seen tonight, he was sure that she could.

The rest of the night passed peacefully, but that hardly made up for what had happened earlier. Longarm was still tired when he crawled out of his blankets, even though the sun was up. Now that it was light, Harriet had built a fire and had put a pot of coffee on to boil. The smell coming from it helped Longarm pry his eyes open.

"I know we should have been on the trail by now," Harriet said before Longarm could comment on the lateness of the hour. "But I thought after everything that happened, we really needed some coffee and a good hot breakfast."

"I ain't arguing with that," Longarm told her. Gratefully, he took the cup of steaming Arbuckle's that she handed him.

Uncle Dan crawled out of the wagon a few minutes later. "How's your head?" Harriet asked him.

"Feels like somebody's nailin' up shingles on the inside of it," he said as he squinted against the light. "I reckon I'll live, though. This ol' noggin o' mine is pretty dadgummed hard."

With his coffee in one hand and the Winchester in the other, Longarm walked around the rock and disturbed some buzzards that were already feasting on the corpses. He grimaced and waved the rifle at the ugly birds as they squawked and flapped awkwardly into the sky.

Now that he could take a better look at the dead men in daylight, he still didn't recognize either of them . . . although the fact that the buzzards had already been at their faces probably didn't help matters. Still, Longarm was reasonably confident that he had never seen either of the men before, which supported his hunch that they were hired guns.

Unfortunately, the coffee didn't taste quite as good after that and his appetite wasn't as keen, either.

He ate anyway, knowing it was never wise to pass up a meal. Then while Harriet and Uncle Dan got ready to travel, he saddled his roan and went looking for the horses that had been ridden by the would-be killers. He found the boot prints left by the Coltmen as they snuck up on the camp and by following them he backtracked to the spot about half a mile to the west where two horses had been left picketed in a little hollow where some sparse grass grew.

Longarm took the horses back to the wagon and tied their reins to the rear of the vehicle. A fella never knew when he might need some extra mounts.

Before they pulled out, he went through the saddlebags on the two horses, finding nothing but some supplies.

"Are you sure you're up to handling the team?" Harriet asked Uncle Dan as the old-timer started to climb onto the wagon seat.

"Sure, I'm fine as frog hair," he said, but as he started to pull himself up, he wobbled, lost his grip, and then fell backward.

Longarm was there to catch him under the arms and keep him from sprawling to the ground. "Take it easy, Uncle Dan," he said as he helped the old-timer straighten up. "Maybe you'd better let Harriet drive the wagon today."

"I just got a mite dizzy for a second," Uncle Dan protested, but then he relented with a shrug. "Reckon it wouldn't hurt anything for me to take it a mite easier today. I ain't as young as I once was, you know."

Harriet tied her horse to the back of the wagon, too, and climbed onto the seat. Uncle Dan sat beside her, clutching his scattergun. "Leastways I can still ride shot-gun," he declared.

"That's right," Longarm agreed with a nod. He swung up into the saddle again. "Let's go."

They set off following the tracks of the outlaw gang that had raided Marathon and doubtless robbed the bank in Ozona before that. Time and wind had begun to erode the hoofprints somewhat, but not to the point that Longarm had any trouble making them out.

Before the morning was over, though, what he had worried would happen did. The trail crossed a long stretch of rocky ground that didn't take prints. That didn't mean it was impossible to follow; the horseshoes of the mounts ridden by their quarry still left marks, little nicks and shiny spots on the rocks, but it was a lot more difficult and time-consuming to read sign like that. Longarm had to dismount and lead his horse, moving forward only a few feet at a time as his eyes searched for the tell tale marks. Their progress the rest of that day was slow and frustrating.

Late in the afternoon, the trail began angling toward the west, which brought them closer to the Santiago Mountains. They camped in the foothills and then the next morning headed for a pass through the rugged peaks. Longarm hadn't lost the trail, but he knew that following it was only going to get more difficult.

Uncle Dan reclaimed the reins of the team today, but Longarm suggested that Harriet ride with him on the wagon anyway. "We're getting into some rugged country," Longarm said. "Pretty soon we may not be able to take the wagon any farther, so you'd best ride while you can."

It was rugged country, as he had said, but in its own way it was beautiful as well, with rocky, pine-dotted peaks soaring into a deep blue sky and towering over twisting valleys and passes. The terrain was mostly dry, but here and there were pockets of green where a spring bubbled out of the rocks and grass and scrubby trees grew.

They were approaching one such little oasis when Longarm heard an odd sound. It took a few seconds for him to realize it was the blatting of goats.

Tag heard it, too, and bounded forward, barking. His natural herding instincts were coming out. Longarm trotted the roan ahead, following the big mutt.

He rounded a bend in the trail and saw a small shack made of branches cut from the pines up on the slopes. The hut sat next to a tiny pond formed by a spring. A little creek trickled from the pond and ran maybe fifty yards along a narrow canyon before it petered out. The mouth of that canyon was closed off by a gate made of brush and poles. The herd of goats was in the canyon, penned there by the gate.

From the looks of it, the goats had been chewing on that gate and had gnawed away quite a bit of it. They would be able to push through it before too much longer.

Longarm frowned. The goatherd who lived in the shack would have nearly a full-time job keeping the gate repaired so the blatting varmints wouldn't wander off. The fact that the gate hadn't been tended to lately didn't bode well.

He looked over his shoulder and saw that the wagon was just coming into sight. He took off his hat, waved it over his head to get the attention of Harriet and Uncle Dan, and called to them, "Stay there!"

Uncle Dan brought the team to a halt. Longarm could tell that they were puzzled about why he was stopping them, but at least they did what he told them. He turned back to the shack and rode forward slowly, drawing the Winchester from the saddle boot as he did so.

Tag stood by the gate, barking at the goats. He wanted to get among them and herd them back and forth, Longarm thought. "Hush up, Tag," he told the dog as he rode up to the shack. Tag ignored him and kept barking, of course.

Holding the Winchester ready, Longarm swung down from the saddle. The door of the hut was open an inch or two. He called, "Anybody home?" When there was no answer, he put the muzzle of the rifle against the door and shoved it open, then stepped back quickly and leveled the rifle, his finger tense on the trigger in case shots erupted from inside the ramshackle little structure.

The only thing that came out of the shack was a weak voice. "*S-señor . . . por favor . . .*"

Longarm moved closer to the door again and said, "This better not be a trick, amigo."

"Please . . . please help . . . *señor . . .*"

Longarm stepped inside. His eyes took a second to adjust to the dimness, even though light came through cracks in the walls of the hut and slanted across its interior. The one room was small, with barely enough room for a crudely made table, a stool, and a bunk on the far wall.

A man lay on that bunk, half propped up. Stripes of sunlight cut across his body. An ancient pistol lay on the

125

tangled blankets beside him, but he made no move toward it. Longarm wasn't sure if the rusty old hogleg would fire anyway.

The hut's lone occupant was a Mexican with dark hair and a shaggy mustache. He wore the white shirt and pants common to border country peasants, but the shirt had a large dark stain on it that could only be blood.

"What happened to you, old son?" Longarm asked as he came closer. From the looks of it, the Mexican goatherd was wounded and didn't represent any threat. Longarm laid the Winchester on the table as he approached. Then he knelt next to the bunk.

"Hombres . . . *malo* hombres . . ."

Bad men, thought Longarm. He figured he knew who the Mexican was talking about.

"Many of them . . . they butcher some of . . . my goats . . . I tried to stop them, but . . . they shot me . . ."

"Take it easy," Longarm told him. He lifted the shirt. The bloodstain on it was dry and stiff, probably a couple of days old. The wound underneath the shirt had bled freely and the skin around the bullet hole was red and puffy where it was tightly swollen. The fella was in bad shape and it was a miracle he had lived this long.

"*Malo* hombres . . ." the wounded man muttered again.

"Damn right they're bad men," Longarm agreed. The gang had already left a path of death and destruction across West Texas and now they had added to it again. "How many were there?"

He wasn't sure the goatherd was coherent enough to answer the question, but after a moment the man said, "*Deis y cinco . . . deis y seis . . .*"

Fifteen or sixteen . . . So the whole gang was still together, thought Longarm. They had stopped here to butcher some goats and have themselves a little feast, and when this fella had tried to stop them, they'd gunned him

126

down. The Mexican must have crawled back in here after the outlaws left.

"Did they say where they were going?" Longarm hated to question the man like this, but he knew there was little or nothing he could do to help him.

"I . . . do not know . . . *un hombre* said something about . . . El Solitario . . ."

The Solitary, Longarm thought. One Who Stands Alone. He knew what the goatherd was talking about.

And it was a gateway to Hell.

Chapter 15

The Mexican goatherd died a few minutes later, before Longarm could do anything to ease his suffering. It was as if the reason the man had clung to life this long was so that he could pass along the knowledge of who had done this to him and where they were going.

Now it was up to Longarm to do something about it.

He stepped out of the shack and used the Winchester to motion to Harriet and Uncle Dan, waving for them to come on. By the time the wagon wheels creaked to a stop outside, Longarm had wrapped the goatherd's body in the bloodstained blanket that had been underneath it. He lifted the bundle and carried it outside. The man didn't seem to weigh much more than a bunch of sticks.

And in the end, that was pretty much what was left of a fella, Longarm thought grimly.

"Oh, no," Harriet said when she saw what he was carrying. "Another one?"

"The man who took care of those goats in the pen over yonder," Longarm explained. "The gang stopped here to kill some goats and cook them. This poor hombre should've let them do whatever they wanted, but he lost his head and tried to stop them. All it got him was a bullet."

"That bunch prob'ly would've killed him anyway," Uncle Dan said.

Longarm nodded and placed the corpse on the ground. The old-timer was likely right about that.

"He was still alive when I got here and before he passed on he was able to give me a lead to where the outlaws are headed."

"Where?" Harriet asked.

"A place called El Solitario."

"Is that a town?"

Longarm shook his head. "Nope. It used to be a volcano, I reckon."

Harriet's eyes widened. "Another volcano?"

"Was a time when there were a heap of 'em in this part of the country," Longarm said. "El Solitario is off to the southwest of here, on the other side of the mountains. Its fire went out a long time ago, maybe thousands of years, and the top of it sort of fell in to form a crater. Although the right name for it is a caldera, I reckon."

Harriet frowned at him. "How do you know things like that?"

"I read a lot, especially when it's close to payday and my wages are all gone." He didn't mention the fact that he was a mite sweet on one of the female clerks at the Denver Public Library, a pretty little blond-headed gal who, like Harriet, wore spectacles. The difference was that she really needed them to see.

Despite the fact that there was a spring here and some grass, the ground was too rocky for grave-digging. Longarm opened the gate and carried the goatherd's blanket-wrapped body up the canyon. He found a narrow little ravine where he was able to place the body and cover it with rocks and brush. That was the best he could do.

"I hope you meant to let them goats loose," Uncle Dan said when Longarm got back. "They scattered hell-west and crosswise, and I ain't roundin' 'em up. It's been my experience that goats is damn near the stupidest critters on the face of the earth."

"No, that's ducks," Longarm said, "but goats run 'em a close second. They just seem dumber because they're bigger. The way they were eating that gate, they would have been loose in another day or two anyway. They can run wild and the ones that the mountain lions don't get will likely stay around here for the grass and the water."

"There are mountain lions in these mountains?" Harriet asked.

Longarm nodded. "Some, but chances are if you don't bother them, they won't bother you."

Harriet didn't look particularly reassured, but she didn't say anything else about the mountain lions.

"How do we get to this El Solitario place?" Uncle Dan asked.

Longarm pointed toward the pass above them. "We'll keep going through Persimmon Gap. On the other side of the Santiagos are a couple of smaller ranges, the Rocillos and the Christmas Mountains. We can make it through them without much trouble and just beyond them we come to the One Who Stands Alone."

"You ever been there?"

Longarm shook his head and said, "No, but I've talked to folks who have. It's a damned big hill, maybe a couple of thousand feet high and nine or ten miles across. The only way to get inside is through some little canyons that cut through the old walls of the volcano. Once you get in, though, it's not so bad. There's enough grass to graze horses, and *tinajas* to catch rainwater. It'd be a natural hide-out for somebody who didn't want folks stumbling over them. There are a few ranches down in the Big Bend, but damn few people."

"Do you think we can get in there?" Harriet asked.

"We should be able to. I can find the way, I reckon.

Likely we can't take the wagon with us, but we've got extra mounts. Can you sit a saddle, Uncle Dan?"

"You just try me and see!" the old-timer snapped. "I was sittin' a saddle all day and half the night when your ma was still changin' your didy!"

"What will we do when we get there?" Harriet wanted to know. "We can't fight that whole gang. There are too many of them."

"That's right, but once we're sure they're in there, I can stay and keep an eye on them while you and Uncle Dan go for help. It's not far from there on down to Presidio. There's talk of building a spur line from the Texas and New Orleans Railroad down to the Rio Grande and they've already put in a telegraph line to Presidio. You can wire Dewey Arquette and Colonel Bascomb and anybody else you can think of. Tell 'em to send plenty of men."

Uncle Dan scratched at his tangled beard. "I reckon we could do that, all right. But what if them sidewinders tried to leave whilst we was gone?"

"I'd have to try to stop them," Longarm said. "Remember, there are only a few ways in and out of El Solitario. A good man with a rifle might be able to keep those outlaws bottled up in there for a while."

"Sounds like it could work, all right," Uncle Dan agreed.

"Or get you killed," Harriet said worriedly to Longarm.

"Let's wait until we're sure they're in there before we go to fretting too much," Longarm said. "Maybe we won't even find them."

"Yes, we will." Harriet was adamant. "And when we do, they're going to tell us what happened to Lieutenant Morgan and the rest of that cavalry patrol."

Longarm nodded. That was the whole idea of tracking down the outlaw gang.

He just hoped the news wouldn't be too bad, once they caught up to those owlhoots.

• • •

The next couple of days were exhausting, but at least nobody tried to kill them during that time. They were able to get the wagon through the pass at Persimmon Gap but then had to leave it as they worked their way farther west. They parked the vehicle under an overhang in a canyon and unhitched the team. When Harriet asked what they would do with all the supplies, Uncle Dan said, "I've packed mules before. We'll cut up that canvas cover and rig alforjas out of the pieces. We got enough hosses we can carry pert' near ever'thing from the wagon and then come back for it later, when this is all over."

That made sense to Longarm, too. They had eight horses, enough for pack animals and spare saddlers, so they might as well use them.

They followed game trails through the Christmas Mountains and the Rocillos. A couple of times Longarm pointed out mountain lions on the slopes well above them. The big cats made no move to attack them, just sat with their tails switching back and forth and watched the humans pass by. Tag growled deep in his throat as he looked up at the mountain lions.

"I reckon you wouldn't want to tangle with those pussycats, old son," Longarm told him with a grin.

By the third day he could tell that the trek was taking its toll on his companions. Despite Uncle Dan's bluster, he was getting on in years and even though he seemed to have recovered from getting walloped on the head, he was growing exhausted. As for Harriet, though she rode well enough, she wasn't accustomed to spending day after day in the saddle. She groaned a little as her sore muscles protested whenever she dismounted.

Longarm was holding up well. He was all rawhide to start with and he had spent much of his life tracking down owlhoots. But he had to admit that even he felt a little relief when he spotted El Solitario that morning.

He called a brief halt and pointed out the ancient volcano. "That's where we're headed," he told the others.

"There's no chance of that volcano erupting, is there?" Harriet asked with a worried frown.

"I ain't no scientist, so I don't give no guarantees, but I think the chance of it is mighty slim. It probably hasn't been active for thousands of years."

"What happened with that other volcano you mentioned?"

"It just sat there and didn't do a dadgummed thing." Longarm smiled as he remembered how he had used some dynamite and brush fires to make it *seem* that the volcano was erupting, but he didn't mention that. Nor did he say anything about the other volcano not far across the border that really had erupted a few years earlier and nearly swallowed up his friend Jessie Starbuck. No point in worrying Harriet even more.

After that short rest, they pushed on. By the end of the day, they were close enough to El Solitario so that it dominated the entire southwestern horizon. Longarm took out his field glasses and studied the wall of stone. He saw a dark slash that marked one of the canyons leading into the caldera.

"What if the gang ain't in there?" Uncle Dan asked.

"Then we've had a ride over here for nothing and we'll have to go back and pick up the trail again."

"Might be harder now," the old-timer pointed out.

"Maybe," Longarm said with a shrug. "All life's a gamble, ain't it?"

"You got that right."

They made camp at a tiny spring. Waterholes had grown scarce the past couple of days. By and large, this was mighty dry country and Longarm figured it would be best to fill up all their canteens while they had the chance.

A ridge thrust itself up above their campsite. That evening Longarm took his Winchester and climbed up there to have a look around. For all that he could see, they might have been completely alone in this rocky wilderness, the only human beings for thousands of miles.

He knew that wasn't true, of course. Twenty miles or so to the south was a ranch, and beyond it were the settlements of Presidio and Lajitas, both of them founded by the Spanish who had first colonized this region. A fella didn't have to get far from those settlements, though, before it seemed like he was on the back side of the moon.

He heard someone coming and looked around to see Harriet climbing toward him. When she reached the top of the ridge, she sat down beside him on a slab of rock and looked around. "It's beautiful up here . . . in an ugly sort of way."

Longarm chuckled. He knew exactly what she meant.

"How do we proceed from here?" she asked.

"Tomorrow, you and Uncle Dan wait here while I take a pasear over to the Solitary One and have a look-see inside."

"You're going by yourself?"

"I reckon that's best."

"Well, I'm not sure I do," she said. "What if something happens to you? If the outlaws are in there, they might catch you."

"I'm a pretty fair hand at skulkin' around," Longarm assured her. "I don't intend to get caught."

"Nobody intends for bad things to happen to them. But they do anyway."

"If I don't come back, you can be sure that something has happened to me. In that case, the two of you hightail it for Presidio and holler for help."

"Leaving you alone?"

"By then, likely you won't have to worry about me."

She looked at him for a long moment and then said, "If you're trying to reassure me, Custis, you're doing a mighty poor job of it."

135

He slipped an arm around her shoulders. "How about this, then?" As she turned her face up to his, he kissed her.

Her lips parted, inviting his tongue to explore the hot, wet cavern of her mouth. She molded her body against him, the soft pillows of her breasts pressing into his side. He reached over and cupped the left one, teasing the nipple into hardness with his thumb. He stroked it through the fabric of her shirt.

After a few moments, she broke the kiss and pulled back slightly, just enough to be able to unbutton her shirt and spread it open. She pulled his head down to her bosom, cradling it for a moment in the valley between her breasts. He kissed the silky skin there and gradually worked his way along the slope of her left breast to the nipple. His tongue circled hotly around it and then his lips closed over it as he began to gently suck.

Harriet stroked his hair and closed her eyes in pleasure as he sucked and kissed and licked both of her breasts. Up here on the ridge, they were out of sight of the camp, so they didn't have to worry about Uncle Dan seeing them.

Longarm's shaft was hard. Harriet caressed it through his trousers while he tongued and sucked her nipples. After a while, she unfastened the buttons of his fly and freed his manhood. Both of her hands stroked up and down its rigid length.

"Let me do something for you, Custis," she whispered.

Longarm was glad to indulge that request. He sat up and braced himself a little better on the rock as she lowered her head over his groin. Holding the shaft in both hands, she licked all around the head and lapped up the moisture she milked from the opening at its tip.

Then she opened her mouth wide and wrapped her lips around it, taking in the whole broad head. She ran her tongue around the crown and the hot sweetness of her mouth made Longarm groan quietly. She sucked lightly as she gradually swallowed more and more of him.

Longarm felt excitement building in him as she skill-fully used her mouth on him. From what she had said, he judged that she wanted to finish him off this way. That was more than all right with him. He wanted to spend his seed in her mouth.

She must have sensed that his climax was rising within him. Her lips tightened on him as she began to suck harder. Longarm tangled his fingers in her red hair. His hips lifted slightly from the rock. Harriet made little noises of encouragement.

Longarm's culmination burst from him, shooting into her mouth and down her throat in white-hot spurts. He shuddered as he emptied himself in spasm after spasm. Harriet swallowed eagerly, taking everything he had to give her.

When she had drained the last of his climax, she gave his shaft a final squeeze and lick, then snuggled against him with his arm tight around her shoulders. They sat there like that as the red-orange glow left over from the sunset began to fade in the western sky.

That had been a mighty nice moment, Longarm thought.

He hoped it didn't turn out to be Harriet's final good-bye to him.

Chapter 16

The next morning Longarm picked out the best of the horses and saddled it for the ride to El Solitario. He put plenty of food and ammunition in the saddlebags and hung two full canteens on the horse as well. Then he turned to Harriet and Uncle Dan and said, "If I'm not back by the end of the day tomorrow, you can figure I'm not coming back. That's when you head for Presidio and send those wires to the authorities."

"What if we hear shooting?" Harriet asked. Her face was tight with worry.

"Then don't wait," Longarm told her. "Light a shuck for Presidio right then and there." He had given both of them good directions for how to reach the border settlement and he was confident they could make it.

"Shouldn't we come to help you instead?" Harriet persisted.

Longarm shook his head. "That'd be the worst thing you could do. If I'm still alive—and that'll be a mighty big if—I'll be a prisoner. You wouldn't stand a chance of getting me out of there, just the two of you. That'd take a company of cavalry or a mighty big posse . . . or both."

"He's right, gal," Uncle Dan said to Harriet.

"I know, I know." She shook her head. "I just have a bad feeling about this."

"Well, I hope your hunch is wrong," Longarm told her. He swung up into the saddle and then nodded to them. "So long."

He rode away, leaving them there with Tag . . . a woman, an old man, and a dog. He hoped they would all be there, still safe and sound, when he got back.

Hell, he hoped he got back safely himself, he thought with a wry grin.

This was some of the most rugged country in the world. Ancient upheavals had thrust up long spiny ridges in the earth. The weathering of the passing centuries had smoothed them out a little, but they were still pretty much useless . . . unless you were an owlhoot looking for a place to hide from the law. Longarm spotted a few cows here and there, gaunt old mavericks who had probably inhabited the draws and ravines between the ridges for years. It wouldn't be worth the time and trouble it would take to haze them out of the badlands.

El Solitario loomed larger and larger in front of him. He was careful not to skyline himself as he approached the old volcano. If the gang's hide-out was in the caldera, they probably had lookouts posted to watch for anyone coming near the place. Longarm stayed out of sight as much as possible.

He was only a few hundred yards from the base of the volcano when he heard shots. The gun blasts didn't come from the stony slopes in front of him, as he might have expected if he had been spotted.

They came from *behind* him.

He stiffened in the saddle and turned around sharply, peering back the way he had come.

There was only one explanation for that gunfire. Someone had stumbled over the camp where Harriet and Uncle

Dan were waiting. Someone hostile. Members of the outlaw gang they were tracking, more than likely.

Longarm wheeled the horse and raced back toward the camp.

Fear for the safety of his two companions was uppermost in his mind at first, but as he rode hard toward the northeast, reason reasserted itself. He reined the horse to a halt and listened intently.

The rugged landscape was quiet again except for the faint keening of the wind. No more shots disturbed the silence.

That meant the fight was over, Longarm thought grimly. Either Harriet and Uncle Dan had been victorious and didn't need his help anymore, or they had been killed or captured. Whichever it was, he didn't need to go busting back in there like a crazy man.

Chances were, if the outlaws were on their way to El Solitario, they would pass somewhere close to where he was. He looked around, spotted a brush-choked ravine with a cluster of boulders at its entrance, and dismounted to lead the horse toward it. He needed to get out of sight.

Waiting was hard, damned hard. A part of him still wanted to rush back to the campsite and see what had happened to Harriet and Uncle Dan. But if they were still alive, he would have a much better chance to help them if he stayed out of the outlaws' hands himself. He just had to be patient.

That patience was rewarded a short time later when he heard the ringing sound of horseshoes on stony ground. Longarm drew back deeper into the gulch. He stood tensely, one hand clamped over his horse's nose to keep the animal from making any noises as the other horses passed by.

The riders came in sight, moving slowly around a large pinnacle of rock that thrust up into the sky. Three men, riding side by side, and as Longarm got a good look at them, his eyes widened in shock.

They wore black campaign caps, blue shirts, and blue trousers with yellow stripes down the legs . . . the uniform of United States cavalry troopers.

Longarm almost stepped out of the ravine and called to them, but something held him back. A second later he was grateful for that instinct, because more riders came into view. Longarm's heart slugged harder in his chest as he recognized Harriet Summers and Uncle Dan Boldin. Harriet seemed to be unhurt, but the old-timer had a bloody rag bound around his left arm. A line of blood ran down the side of his face, too, from a gash on his forehead. Both of them were unarmed.

Three more cavalrymen brought up the rear behind the two prisoners. They carried Spencer repeating rifles pointed in the general direction of Harriet and Uncle Dan and their stance made it clear they would shoot if the captives tried to get away.

Longarm's brain was whirling from these unexpected developments, but he thought he had a pretty good idea what was going on. It all made sense now, in a perverse sort of way.

Nobody had been able to find the gang that had been terrorizing West Texas because everyone was looking for outlaws.

No one had thought to look for the cavalry.

It was simple, really. Ride out on a patrol that would last for several weeks. Head for a hide-out where civilian clothes and horses and gear were stashed. Swap the uniforms for range garb, the cavalry mounts for civilian-branded horses, and ride off again, bound for whatever train hold-up or bank robbery was on the agenda. Head back for the hide-out with the loot, cache it there, change back to the cavalry uniforms, and no one would ever believe that these troopers were really desperadoes. Longarm could have kicked himself for not putting it together sooner.

But he knew he had had no reason to suspect that the

lost patrol and the outlaw gang were one and the same. Everything he had been told about Lieutenant Scott Morgan and the other missing men had indicated that they were good soldiers.

The question now was what to do about the situation. He was outnumbered six to one and Harriet and Uncle Dan were prisoners. If he jumped the group of crooked troopers, there was a good chance one or both of them would be hit by flying lead. As much as he hated to admit it, Longarm knew that his best course might be to bide his time and wait for a better opportunity to free his friends.

And in the meantime, if he followed the cavalrymen, they would lead him right to the hide-out.

The group rode past the gulch without ever glancing toward Longarm. He waited until they were several hundred yards away and then moved out after them.

Again he had to fight the urge to attack. He could probably down the three men riding behind Harriet and Uncle Dan before they knew what hit them.

But if he did that, the other three would whirl around and start slinging lead, and the two prisoners would be caught in the cross fire. Patience, hard though it might be, was the best thing at the moment.

Just as Longarm expected, the little group of riders headed straight for El Solitario and that canyon he had seen earlier and marked as a likely entrance to the huge heap of stone. Longarm hung back quite a ways, using whatever cover he could and being careful not to expose himself to a casual backward glance.

When he saw the riders enter the canyon, he reined to a halt, knowing that if he came any closer, he risked being seen by a lookout posted near the entrance. He would have to wait for nightfall to approach the hide-out.

In the meantime, a lot of hours would go by. Long, frustrating hours when anything might be happening in there to Harriet and Uncle Dan.

Longarm found some shade under an overhanging bluff, picketed his horse, and drowsed through the heat of the day. Although he was worried about his two companions, he was able to push that into a corner of his mind and rest. The worry never completely stopped gnawing at his brain, however.

At midday he chewed some jerky from his saddlebags and washed it down with water from one of the canteens. Then he went back to waiting.

Finally the sun lowered in the western sky until it seemed to be sitting on top of the ancient volcano. As it slipped down even more, Longarm saddled up and rode toward the Solitary One. He had kept an ear open all during the long day and he hadn't heard any gunshots coming from the hide-out.

That didn't mean something else bad couldn't have happened, but at least it was cause for a little hope.

He took his time, letting the sun go down so that shadows shrouded the land as he approached. Before he reached the canyon he reined in and dismounted, tying the horse's reins to a scrubby, gnarled bush. He took the Winchester from the saddle boot and patted the animal's shoulder, then started off on foot. He moved quietly, using all the stealth that his years of experience had taught him.

Only the faintest glow of rose remained in the sky as Longarm entered the canyon. Inside the narrow declivity, the darkness was complete. He had to feel his way along slowly. Only as the stars gradually appeared in the black velvet heavens did enough silvery illumination filter down for him to be able to see a little.

He wasn't far inside the canyon when he heard someone cough. Freezing where he was, Longarm looked around and after a moment he spotted a tiny red glow that marked the end of a quirly as a guard sucked on it. The glow was on the left-hand side of the canyon, about twenty feet off the ground. There had to be a ledge up there where the guard was posted, Longarm thought.

Carefully, Longarm moved over until he was underneath the ledge. He bent and felt around until he found a small rock. Then he tossed it toward the center of the canyon. It landed and rolled away with a clatter.

"Who's there?" the guard called from the ledge.

The hombre wasn't overly blessed with brains. He had just announced where he was and an enemy could have opened fire on him, aiming at his voice.

Longarm didn't want any gunshots to warn the outlaws in the caldera that something was wrong, so he just stood there with his back pressed against the canyon wall, motionless and silent, and waited.

He heard boot leather scraping on rock and knew the sentry must be coming down to check on the noise. Longarm followed the sounds, sliding along the rock wall. There had to be a trail leading down from the ledge, even though he couldn't see it. He intended to intercept the guard at the foot of that trail.

A whiff of tobacco smoke drifted to his nose. The guard shouldn't have been smoking in the first place. Discipline must be a little lax in the gang, Longarm told himself. That could prove to be a slight advantage, but probably not enough to offset the high odds against him.

One bite of the apple at a time, he thought. First he had to deal with this son of a bitch.

The guard stumbled a little and mumbled a curse as he reached the bottom of the trail. Longarm knew from the sounds that the outlaw was only a few feet in front of him. He struck hard and fast, smashing the butt of the rifle at the back of the guard's head.

Unfortunately, some instinct must have warned the man, because he twisted aside suddenly and the blow landed on his shoulder instead. He cried out in pain and lurched toward Longarm.

Suddenly, the big lawman found himself locked in a desperate struggle in the darkness. Fearing that the guard would pull his six-gun and fire a warning shot, Longarm reached toward the man's hip. His fingers wrapped around the guard's wrist and clamped down, stopping the draw just short of the butt of the holstered revolver.

But at the same time, the guard's other hand groped for Longarm's neck and found it. Knobby-knuckled fingers tightened in a brutal, choking grip. The guard drew in a deep breath.

Longarm knew the man was about to yell. Such a shout in this narrow canyon would echo loudly and the sound would reach into the caldera where the rest of the outlaws would hear it. Longarm struck with the Winchester again, slashing the barrel across the guard's face. The man staggered but kept his death grip on Longarm's throat.

Longarm thrust out a leg and hauled hard on the man's wrist. The guard tripped and went down, falling over Longarm's leg. That still didn't tear loose his hold on Longarm's neck. The lawman was pulled down, too. The rifle slipped out of his other hand and clattered away.

Over and over the men rolled on the stony ground. Longarm couldn't throw a punch because if it missed, he would smash his fist against the rocks and probably break several bones in it. He had to grapple with the guard instead. He managed to twist the man's arm behind him and as Longarm gave it a hard wrench, he heard bones pop. He didn't know if it was the elbow or the shoulder that had come out of its socket, but one of them surely had. Longarm clamped his other hand over the man's mouth just in time to stifle the agonized yell.

The guard tried to bite him. Longarm jerked his hand away. The outlaw's teeth clicked together futilely. Longarm grabbed him by the throat and rolled over, putting the guard under him. His knee rose, slamming into the man's groin. The man grunted and spasmed as blinding pain shot through him. His choking hand fell away from Longarm's throat at last. While the guard was stunned, Longarm pulled his head up and then smashed it against the ground. The outlaw went limp.

Longarm pushed himself up and off the unconscious guard. He checked the man's pulse, found it rapid and erratic. That final blow of the guard's head against the ground might have fractured his skull.

Even though he was confident that the guard wouldn't be waking up any time soon, if ever, Longarm didn't take any chances. As he felt the guard's body, searching him for weapons, he found that the man was dressed in range clothes, not a cavalry uniform. He used the man's belt to tie his hands behind his back and stuffed a bandanna into his mouth as a gag.

When the outlaw was secure, Longarm felt around until he located the Winchester he had dropped. Evidently only one guard was on duty in the canyon at a time; if there had been another, by now the unavoidable noises of the fracas would have brought him to check on his comrade. Longarm didn't think the racket had been loud enough to reach to the hide-out, though.

He took a deep breath and catfooted on down the canyon, moving deeper into the ancient hellhole known as El Solitario.

Chapter 17

By the time Longarm reached the end of the canyon, where it opened out into the caldera, the moon had risen so that he had a pretty good look at the scene before him.

El Solitario was about nine miles in diameter, he recalled, but he had walked for more than a mile through the canyon. Allowing for the thickness of the walls, the caldera itself was about six miles across and mostly flat, although some areas were cut by ravines and knife-edge ridges. *Tinajas*, or natural cisterns, caught and held rainwater and there were a few spring-fed pools as well. Grass grew here and there, enough to support deer and mountain goats and the occasional longhorn that wandered in from outside.

For the most part, though, El Solitario was a world unto itself, seldom visited from outside. A perfect hiding place for outlaws who didn't want to be bothered.

Longarm stood for several minutes in the darkness at the mouth of the entrance canyon and looked and listened. He didn't see any sign of human habitation. He was going to have to venture deeper into the caldera to locate the hide-out.

Carrying the Winchester, he walked toward the center of the vast depression in the earth. As he did, he couldn't help but imagine what it had been like when this had been an active volcano, miles wide, spewing flame and smoke and molten rock out into the primordial world in which it existed. He knew some scientists speculated that at different times, what was now West Texas had been covered by an ocean, and then a steaming jungle, and finally volcanoes like El Solitario.

He was glad he hadn't had to hunt down owlhoots back in those days. West Texas was bad enough the way it was now.

The moon rose higher, a bright yellow orb staring down from the night sky, as Longarm explored the caldera. After about an hour, he heard horses whinnying not far off. He followed the sound and soon found a corral built of poles cut from the stubby mesquite trees that dotted the floor of the depression. A couple of dozen horses milled around inside the corral.

Beyond the enclosure squatted several cabins made of mud, stone, and adobe. This was it, Longarm thought, the headquarters of the outlaw gang that had ranged far and wide over West Texas, looting and killing.

And in one of those cabins, Harriet and Uncle Dan were probably being held prisoner. If he could find them, dispose of their guards, and then get out of here without being discovered, they still had a chance to trap the gang. At the moment, however, Longarm would settle for freeing Harriet and Uncle Dan. He could go after the outlaws again later if he had to.

One of the cabins was dark, but light showed in the windows of the other three. Longarm headed for the darkened one first. As he approached, he spotted a man sitting on a stool in front of the closed door. A rifle rested across his legs as he sat there and sucked on a quirly. The presence of the guard supported Longarm's guess that the prisoners were inside that darkened cabin.

Laughter came from one of the other buildings. The outlaws were happy, no doubt celebrating their latest suc-

150

cessful foray into crime. As Longarm crouched behind a rock, he wondered why they had abandoned their practice of masquerading as a cavalry patrol. By not returning to Fort Stockton as they had all the other times, they had aroused worry and curiosity and in the end that disappearance was responsible for setting Longarm on their trail.

Maybe they were tired of pretending to be honest soldiers. If they had enough loot stashed here they could have decided that the ruse was no longer worth the trouble. Longarm didn't really care about the reasons for their actions; he just wanted to bring their lawlessness to a halt. After rescuing Harriet and Uncle Dan, of course . . .

More laughter and loud voices came from the cabins. The festivities were getting raucous. The guard in front of the door stood up and paced back and forth for a moment, then stopped and glared toward the other buildings. Judging from his stance, Longarm thought he must resent being stuck guarding the prisoners when the rest of the gang was whooping it up and probably getting drunk.

A new sound came from one of the lighted cabins: the shrill laugh of a woman. Longarm frowned. That hadn't sounded like Harriet and anyway he couldn't think of any reason she would be laughing right now. Another woman joined in the hilarity.

Had to be some soiled doves brought up from one of the border settlements, Longarm decided. That was the only explanation. He didn't know how many women might be here in the hide-out. If it came down to shooting, he would try to see to it that none of them were hurt, but that couldn't be his main worry. They had to know these men were outlaws, so to a certain extent they would just have to take their chances.

Staying a good fifty yards away, he circled the darkened cabin and saw that it had no windows. The only way in and out was the door where the outlaw stood guard. Longarm wondered if he could decoy the sentry away from the door.

He was about to give it a try when a man emerged from one of the other cabins. He weaved slightly as he walked, showing the effects of the whiskey he'd likely been guzzling, but he wasn't too unsteady on his feet as he strode toward the darkened cabin. He was tall, broad-shouldered, and burly, and a derby hat sat on his head. Longarm recalled the description of the leader of the gang that had raided Marathon. He figured he was looking at the boss outlaw.

The guard came to his feet and said, "Something wrong, Coley?" His voice carried clearly to where Longarm was now hidden behind a small clump of brush.

"No, nothing wrong," the man called Coley rumbled in reply. He waved a big hand toward the cabin. "Get that red-headed gal out here. It's time she learned she might as well be friendly. If she don't, I'll knock it into that pretty head of hers."

Coley's voice was a little slurred, but not much. He wasn't too drunk to make good on his threat. Longarm gritted his teeth and suppressed the impulse to stand up, draw a bead, and blow the bastard's head off. There was enough moonlight that he felt sure he could make the shot.

But then all hell would break loose and a dozen or more outlaws would come tumbling out of those cabins, ready to start shooting.

"Go on, bring her out here," Coley snapped at the guard. "I ain't got all night, you know." He belched loudly. "Well, actually, I reckon I do. I can take all night with her and by the time I'm done she won't never smart off again."

From the sound of that, Harriet had had a few things to say to her captors. Despite the seriousness of the situation, a faint smile flickered over Longarm's face. Harriet had spirit, all right. That was usually a good thing in a woman.

Tonight, though, it might just get her killed.

The guard turned toward the door. It must have had a padlock on it, because he fumbled in his pocket for a key.

Longarm wondered if he could rush the men while the guard's back was turned, knock out Coley, and then wallop the guard before either man could let out a yell. It was a longshot, of course, but it might be his best chance of getting Harriet and Uncle Dan, as well as himself, out of this hole in the ground with their hides intact.

He tensed his muscles, ready to lunge toward the outlaws, but before he could move several more men came out of one of the other cabins. They were laughing and talking boisterously and passing a jug back and forth.

"Hey, Coley," one of them called. "You ain't gonna hog all that little gal's sweetness to yourself, are you?"

Longarm bit back a curse and crouched lower behind the brush. The odds were too great now. He wouldn't stand a chance of freeing the prisoners without alerting all the other members of the gang.

Coley turned to the newcomers and snapped, "Y'all got women already."

"Just a couple o' Mex whores," one of the men said. "We're tired o' them. We want some o' that fresh stuff, too."

"Well, you ain't gettin' none of it, at least not yet."

One of the other outlaws stalked forward as Coley turned back toward the cabin. "Damn it, you can't hold out on us," he said. "You may be the boss when it comes to the jobs we pull, but here in El Solitario, it's share and share alike, you know that."

"Go on back inside, Burnett," Coley said in a low, dangerous voice. "I ain't arguin' with you about this. I'm tellin' you how it's gonna be."

Burnett grabbed Coley's shoulder. "And I'm tellin' you to go to hell!" he yelled as he jerked the big man in the derby around and threw a punch at him.

Coley pulled free and swayed to the side so that the blow only grazed his ear. He swung a punch of his own, driving a big fist into Burnett's midsection. As Burnett doubled over in pain, Coley clasped his hands together and clubbed them down brutally on the back of Burnett's neck. Burnett fell on his face, out cold.

The men with him weren't going to take this lying down. A couple of them yelled angrily and rushed Coley. The others were right behind them.

Swinging his fists wildly in sledgehammer-like blows, Coley tried to fight them off, but the numbers were against him. His opponents overwhelmed him and brought him down. Several of them sprawled on the ground with him.

Longarm's teeth grated together in frustration. This brawl would have been a perfect distraction . . . if it had taken place somewhere else.

As it was, the struggling men were right in front of the only door into the cabin where the prisoners were being held. Even in the middle of a fight, Longarm wouldn't be able to get past them unnoticed. But maybe when the fracas was over they would all slink away to lick their wounds and he could get back to trying to rescue Harriet and Uncle Dan. Maybe a few of them would even kill each other, if he was really lucky, and cut down the odds against him.

The fight went on for several minutes. Despite being outnumbered, Coley was the biggest and strongest of the outlaws, which was probably the reason he was the leader in the first place. He got his hands on the throats of a couple of the men, banged their heads together, and then threw them into their fellows. He shrugged off the kicks and punches that rained down on him and finally surged back to his feet, shaking off his tormenters like a huge grizzly bear might shake off a pack of wolves. He grabbed one man and used him as a flail to knock down several others. It was an awesome display of strength and Longarm wasn't surprised when Coley's opponents—the ones who were still conscious—drew back away from him.

"That's enough," one of them gasped. "You don't have to kill us, damn it!"

154

"You brought it on yourselves," Coley rumbled. He wiped the back of a hand across his mouth, which was bleeding a little. "Son of a bitch. I need a drink."

He stumbled toward the cabin he had come from.

Longarm held his breath. From the looks of it, Coley had forgotten all about Harriet and the reason he had come over here in the first place. The other men who could still walk picked up the ones who couldn't and followed Coley. Even the guard started in that direction, evidently pretty thirsty himself.

Coley stopped in the lighted doorway of the other cabin and looked back over his shoulder. "Damn it, Ross, get back to where you're supposed to be. You even left the door unlocked, you halfwit! What if them prisoners got out?"

In his hiding place, Longarm seethed. He knew that the guard had unlocked the door, too, and had hoped that everyone else would overlook that little matter. That would have made rescuing Harriet and Uncle Dan mighty easy.

It wasn't to be, though. The guard, Ross, went back and snapped the padlock on the door closed. Then, with a disappointed sigh, he sat down again on the stool and went back to brooding.

All the fight had accomplished was to keep Coley from attacking Harriet right now. Still, that had been a lucky break, and Longarm would take it. The situation wasn't any worse now than it had been before. He could go back to trying to think of some way to decoy the guard away from the door. Longarm needed to jump him, knock him out, and get the key to that padlock, all without making much noise.

A sound behind him made him go even lower on the ground. Sand crunched under someone's boot. One of the outlaws could have gone out to relieve himself or might be walking around for some other reason. Longarm couldn't afford to be discovered now. He lay absolutely still in the shadow thrown by the bush behind which he was hidden.

155

Again he heard a faint sound, but off to his left this time. He turned his head and peered in that direction. After a moment his keen eyes picked out a shape moving over there, a deeper patch of shadow in the night. As he watched, the shape resolved itself into a man and moonlight reflected off the barrel of the revolver the skulker held.

Something was wrong about this, Longarm thought. The man seemed to be sneaking up on the cabin just as he had a short time earlier. Why would one of the outlaws be doing that? They could just walk up to the place openly, especially if they called out first to alert the guard to who they were.

Maybe that fella circling around the cabin *wasn't* one of the gang, Longarm told himself. Which brought up an interesting question.

If he wasn't an outlaw, who the hell was he?

It might pay to find out.

Longarm waited a little longer, then came up on hands and knees and began to crawl after the mysterious stranger. Moving as silently as a phantom, Longarm followed the man around to the back side of the cabin. The man stopped and studied the little hut, much as Longarm had. He wasn't one of the outlaws, or he wouldn't be acting like this. Longarm was convinced of that.

The enemy of my enemy is my friend, the old saying went, and Longarm believed there was often some truth to that. But he couldn't take a chance. He had to find out exactly who this stranger was, and do it without alerting the owlhoots who were only a few yards away.

He crept silently into position, then came up on his feet and struck the unknown man from behind with the speed of a snake. Thrusting the Winchester in front of him, Longarm reached over his left shoulder and grabbed the barrel, then brought it back hard against the man's throat, choking off any outcry. Longarm twisted, tripping the man and throwing him facedown to the ground. His knee landed in the middle of the man's back and pinned him there. Longarm pressed the rifle upward under his chin. One good yank would break his neck. The man must have realized that, because he lay still instead of fighting. Longarm heard the breath hissing between his clenched teeth.

"Take it easy, old son," Longarm whispered in the man's ear. "Hate to jump you like this, but I got to find out who you are. We may be on the same side. You *sabe*?"

The man's head jerked slightly in as much of a nod as he could manage with that rifle pressed across his throat like an iron bar.

Taking a chance, Longarm whispered, "I'm Deputy U.S. Marshal Custis Long. I'm gonna let off on this Winchester a mite, and you tell me who you are."

The man nodded again and Longarm relaxed the pressure on his throat. But only slightly, and they both knew that Longarm could still kill him in the blink of an eye.

Words came from the man's mouth, between tightly clenched lips and teeth and Longarm leaned forward to listen. What he heard made him stiffen in surprise.

The stranger said, "I'm . . . Lieutenant . . . Scott Morgan!"

Chapter 18

The shock didn't last long. Like the tumblers of a lock clicking into place, one fact after another fell into line in Longarm's head until he had the whole picture clear at last. With lightning speed, he thought through the whole thing and knew what he had to do.

He put his mouth close to his captive's ear and breathed, "Hang on, Lieutenant. I'll let you up. We got to be mighty quiet, though."

He let go of the Winchester's barrel with his left hand and withdrew the rifle from Morgan's neck. Straightening, Longarm stepped back. He leaned down to give Morgan a hand and helped the young officer to his feet.

Then together they faded back into the darkness, moving quickly but quietly as they put some distance between them and the cabin where the prisoners were being held.

They didn't stop until they could talk in low tones without any danger of being overheard by the guard. Morgan rubbed his sore neck and said, "I thought you were going to kill me, Marshal."

"I'm sorry about that," Longarm said. "But I didn't know who you were. When I jumped you, I thought you might be one of them outlaws."

"And I thought *you* were one of them. I figured I was a dead man."

"Reckon we were both wrong. I know I was, because I had it all worked out that you and the troopers who left Fort Stockton with you were really outlaws."

"What?" Morgan exclaimed.

Longarm quickly explained the theory he had formed earlier when he saw that the men who had captured Harriet and Uncle Dan wore cavalry uniforms.

"Those were some of *our* uniforms," Morgan said bitterly. "They were stolen from us by those bastards. I think you were partially right, Marshal. Those men intend to masquerade as members of the U.S. cavalry while they're not carrying out their robberies and killings."

Morgan's voice had a stiff-necked sound, but Longarm figured he couldn't blame the man for being upset. Morgan wore range clothes, Longarm saw in the moonlight, instead of the lieutenant's garb to which he was accustomed. He was about as out of uniform as a soldier could get.

"How did those owlhoots wind up with their hands on your uniforms?" Longarm asked.

"Through treachery," Morgan replied. "We were betrayed. I trusted a man I never should have."

"Who might that be?"

"Sergeant Cole Vance."

Longarm nodded. "Big fella, bald-headed, sports a derby hat?"

"That's him. He always preferred a derby when he wasn't on duty. He led us into a trap."

"From what I heard at the fort, Vance was a career noncom. What made him turn outlaw?"

"A career of low pay and hazardous duty, to hear him tell it. He said he was tired of risking his life, that it was time to cash in. He must have come up with the plan to have the patrol ambushed and steal our uniforms."

Remembering how casually the gang had gunned down people and left others to burn in the bank in Marathon, Longarm asked, "How come you're not dead? Seems to me Vance and his pards wouldn't have wanted to leave any witnesses behind."

"Only a few of us survived the ambush. It was east of here, on the other side of the Santiagos. Vance had suggested we bypass Marathon on our way down to the Big Bend because he'd heard rumors that a band of renegade Apaches had crossed the border. I believed him, of course." Again the bitterness edged into Morgan's voice. "Vance's friends cut down on us as we were riding through a draw. Except for him, everyone in the patrol was either killed or wounded in the first volley. They came in and stripped us of our uniforms, stole our horses, and left us for dead. I was still alive, though, and so were four of the other men. When we all came to, Vance and the others were gone."

Longarm nodded. "You were mighty lucky. That bunch might just as easily have put bullets in all your heads, just to make sure you were dead."

"I know. But when I realized there were five of us still alive, I knew that fate had spared us for a reason." Morgan clenched a fist. "We're going to make Vance pay for what he's done."

That sounded good to Longarm. He nodded and said, "I reckon we're after the same thing, then. But there's one thing you don't know. While some of those owlhoots were out scouting the area around El Solitario earlier today, they ran across Harriet Summers and her great-uncle and grabbed 'em. They're prisoners now in that cabin you were looking at."

"Miss Summers? And Boldin? My God, what are *they* doing down here in this Godforsaken wilderness?"

"They came to look for you, just like I did. Harriet was mighty worried about you when you and the rest of the patrol disappeared."

Morgan scrubbed a hand over his face. "Yes, yes, of course. Harriet . . . Harriet would do that." He looked at Longarm. "We have to save them."

Longarm nodded. "Where are the rest of your men?"

"Back in the canyon that leads into this hellhole. We found one of the outlaws in there. Did you kill him, Marshal?"

"He was dead, was he? He was still breathing when I tied him up." Longarm sighed. "He was on guard duty there in the canyon. I was just trying to knock him out, but I reckon I banged his head a mite too hard on the ground. Wasn't really time to be too careful during the ruckus."

"No great loss. That's just one we won't have to deal with. What do you suggest we do now, Marshal?"

"You say there are five of you, counting you?"

"That's right."

"So we're only outnumbered about three to one." Longarm grinned humorlessly. "That ain't too bad. You have guns?"

"We each have a pistol. Vance and his friends took most of our weapons, of course, but they left a few guns lying under the bodies."

"Where'd you get those duds?"

"We found an abandoned ranch house. The clothes had been left behind by whoever lived there. We found a couple of ropes and some saddles there, too, and were able to lasso some wild horses."

"Sounds like that luck of yours was holding," Longarm commented.

"Yes, but it still took us this long to outfit ourselves and track down those thieves. But I swore I wouldn't go back to Fort Stockton until we had caught up with Vance and his cohorts and brought them to justice." Morgan paused, then said, "You mentioned that you came down here looking for us, Marshal?"

"That's right. I stopped at the fort on other business, and Colonel Bascomb told me about you boys disappearing. He asked me if I'd try my hand at looking for you. I wired my boss in Denver, and he said to go ahead. So here I am."

Morgan grinned in the moonlight. "More good luck. But we still haven't decided what to do."

"We need something to even the odds some more." Longarm thought back. "The gang used dynamite on the bank in Marathon, blew the hell out of the place. If they've got any more of the stuff, I wonder where they're keeping it."

"In the cabins with them, perhaps?" Morgan suggested.

Longarm shook his head. "Nobody with any sense wants to sleep in the same room as a bunch of dynamite. The stuff is too damned touchy for that. It goes off if you look at it crosswise. They'll have it stored someplace safe, but away from the cabins a ways. Close enough they can get to it easy, though."

"Well, let's have a look and see if we can find it," Morgan said. "I would think that would even the odds."

"Dynamite's got a way of doing that, all right," Longarm said dryly.

They began skirting the compound, searching for the place where the rest of the gang's explosives were stored. Of course, the outlaws might not have any more dynamite. But Longarm figured they could determine that fairly quickly.

A few minutes later, Longarm spotted something and pointed it out to Morgan. As they approached, they saw that it was a tiny adobe hut, smaller than the cabins where the outlaws lived. When Longarm saw the small but sturdy structure, he knew they had hit pay dirt.

Silently, he motioned to Morgan that they should advance. No one was standing guard at the hut and the door wasn't locked. Longarm swung the door open carefully, in case the hinges creaked. The hut was only about five feet tall and maybe four feet square, just big enough for a couple of wooden crates to be stacked inside it. Longarm pulled the top off one crate and put his hand into it gingerly, almost as if he expected to find a bunch of rattlesnakes coiled up inside there.

What he found was even more deadly: bundles of cylinders tightly wrapped in greasy paper.

"This is it," he whispered to Morgan. He started pulling the bundles of dynamite out of the box and handing them to the lieutenant. There were half a dozen sticks in each bundle, tied together with twine.

Each man took three of the bundles and Longarm had a box of fuses and blasting caps, too. They pulled back until they were out of earshot of the cabins again. Special tools were used to crimp the blasting caps onto the sticks of dynamite, but lacking those tools Longarm and Morgan did the best they could, cutting up the twine so that they could separate the sticks and tie a cap onto each one.

"I've never worked much with dynamite," Morgan said. "Can we be sure that they'll explode this way?"

"There are more chances of a misfire," Longarm admitted, "but it's the only thing we can do. We'll set a couple of sticks next to each of the cabins. That'll leave us some in reserve in case we need to toss in some more."

"You plan to blow the cabins down?"

Longarm nodded. "I'm hoping that'll shake up those old boys so much that they'll surrender. If they don't . . . well, like I said, we'll still have more dynamite."

Morgan hefted one of the paper-wrapped sticks and said, "I've never fought men with explosives before. I'm not sure I like it."

"Not sure I do, either, but it's about the only chance we've got."

"I can't argue with that. Do you want me to go get the rest of my men?"

Longarm nodded. "Bring 'em back here. We'll spread out around the cabins and be ready if any of the gang rushes out after the blasts go off."

Morgan slipped off into the darkness while Longarm

finished preparing the dynamite. Setting it off was going to be a tricky business, especially timing the fuses so that the explosions came as closely together as possible. With some leftover twine, he tied together three pairs of sticks and twisted the fuses together.

He was worried about those Mexican whores in one of the cabins. He didn't want them to be killed when the dynamite went off. He hoped to avoid that by placing the sticks outside, rather than lighting the fuses and tossing them through the door, which would have been more effective. That would slaughter everyone in the cabins, though, and Longarm was a lawman, not a cold-blooded murderer like the outlaws. He had to give them a chance to surrender. Of course, he hoped the blasts would have them so discombobulated and maybe even wounded that they wouldn't have any choice but to give up.

While Morgan was gone, Longarm kept an eye on the cabin where the prisoners were being held. No one came near it except the guard. Coley—Sergeant Cole Vance— must have changed his mind about assaulting Harriet, figuring it would cause too much of a ruckus among the men unless he turned them loose on her, too. Longarm reckoned the attack had only been postponed, though; Vance would still go after her as soon as he thought he could get away with it.

A tense half-hour went by before Morgan returned with the other four survivors from his cavalry troop. He must have explained to them who Longarm was and what they planned to do, because none of the men had any questions and they didn't argue when Longarm began giving them orders.

He told them to spread out around the cabins, pointing to the darkened one where Harriet and Uncle Dan were being held. "I don't reckon bullets would go through those adobe walls and that door's probably thick enough to stop a slug, too. But just in case, try not to sling too much lead in that direction."

The troopers nodded their understanding.

"Lieutenant Morgan and I are going to put dynamite next to those other cabins," Longarm went on. "When the blasts go off, the outlaws who can still move around are liable to rush out. I'll call on them to surrender, but if they don't throw down their guns right off, you open fire on them."

Again the small circle of men nodded.

"You men have your orders," Morgan said. "Move out."

The soldiers split up and faded away into the shadows. Longarm handed Morgan one of the pairs of dynamite sticks and said, "Put this next to the cabin on the far end. I'll take the other two."

"How do we light the fuses?"

Longarm took a square of lucifers from his pocket, broke off several of the sulfur matches, and handed them to the lieutenant.

"I'll place both of mine first, then light the middle one at the same time you light yours. Once they're burning, I'll hustle over to the other one and get it going, too."

"You'll have to hurry," Morgan warned him.

Longarm nodded. "I know. My second pair won't go off at the same time as the first, but that's all right. Won't be more than a couple of seconds between the blasts."

Morgan took a deep breath and asked, "Are we ready, then?"

"We're ready," Longarm said. He nodded toward the small pile of dynamite sticks on the ground at his feet. "We'll leave the extras here. Head back here as soon as you've got your fuses burning."

Morgan jerked his head in acknowledgment. Then he and Longarm began slipping through the darkness toward the rear of the cabins.

Longarm had both pairs of dynamite sticks in his left hand. He hoped he and Morgan weren't discovered as they went about their explosive work. The last thing they needed right now was a gunfight. If a stray bullet were to hit that dynamite in his hand . . .

Well, there wouldn't be enough left of him to scrape up and bury, he thought.

He put that grisly image out of his head and went down into a crouch as he approached the back of the nearest cabin. Those outlaws were too damned overconfident; that arrogance was going to be their downfall. They probably thought this was such a good hide-out that no law would come within fifty miles of them. They were about to find out just how wrong they were.

Longarm knelt beside the adobe wall and placed the tied-together sticks of dynamite on the ground at the wall's base. He twisted the fuses a little more so that they stuck up in a single strand that would be easy to reach. Then he moved over to the next cabin and repeated the process. He looked at the third cabin and saw the patch of darkness that represented Lieutenant Morgan crouching next to it. Morgan gave a little wave to signify that he was ready.

Longarm used an iron-hard thumbnail to snap a lucifer into life. He held the flame to the tip of the twisted fuses. They caught instantly and began to burn with a sputtering hiss. Longarm leaped to his feet and ran over to the other cabin, hoping to use the same match to light the fuses there. It flickered out before he could do so, however, and he lost a couple of valuable seconds striking another match.

But then the fuses were burning and a glance told him that the others were, too. Longarm dropped the second match, whirled around, and broke into a run. There was no time now to worry about stealth, but no cries of discovery came from the cabins. The outlaws' senses had been dulled by the debauchery they had been up to since returning to the Solitary One.

They were about to get woke up, though . . . with a vengeance.

Chapter 19

The first two explosions went off together, with a sound like a gigantic thunderclap. The blast was strong enough to knock Longarm off his feet, even though he had run at least a hundred yards. Before the echoes had even had a chance to start rolling around the caldera and bouncing off the walls of the old volcano, the second explosion ripped through the night. Longarm had lifted his head and saw the bright flare of the dynamite as it detonated.

Debris from the explosions thudded down around him. Sand and gravel pattered on the ground like rain. While it was still falling, Longarm surged to his feet and raced on to the spot where he and Morgan had left the rest of the dynamite.

When Longarm reached the explosives, he scooped up a couple of the sticks and turned back toward the cabins, ready to light and throw them if he needed to. Morgan stumbled up at that moment, shaking his head.

"That sounded like a battery of cannon going off," the lieutenant said.

"I heard barrages a lot louder and longer than that, back during the war," Longarm said. "Those blasts were loud enough, though."

They had been effective, too. In the moonlight, Long-arm saw that the rear walls of all three cabins had been blown down, and the roofs had collapsed on a couple of them. Clouds of smoke and dust drifted around, obscuring the scene, but Longarm caught glimpses of several men stumbling around.

"This is the law!" he shouted at them. "Drop your guns and elevate! Right now!"

Shots roared out, blending with the dying echoes of the explosions. Longarm saw muzzle flame lick out from the brush around the cabins as the four troopers opened fire. He stiffened as he realized that none of the shots had come from the outlaws. The soldiers had started shooting before the outlaws even had a chance to surrender.

"Tell them to hold their fire," he said tersely to Morgan.

"Cease-fire!" the young officer bellowed. "Cease-fire!"

His men ignored him and kept pouring lead into the area around the cabins. Longarm heard a woman scream in pain. "Damn it!" he grated as he started forward.

Morgan caught hold of his arm, stopping him. "You can't really blame them, Marshal," he said. "They were betrayed and ambushed, shot and left for dead. If it was up to Vance and the others, all of us would have died. It's understandable that they want revenge."

"It ain't understandable that they're disobeying orders," Longarm snapped. "I intend to take that up with Colonel Bascomb when we get back."

Morgan shrugged. "You'll do what you have to do, I suppose."

The shooting became more sporadic. Longarm put the dynamite back on the ground and then watched as the troopers approached the ruined cabins. They looked like phantoms moving through the clouds of smoke and dust. A shot rang out every now and then as a wounded outlaw was finished off. A little muscle jumped in Longarm's tightly clenched jaw every time that happened.

Within minutes, the massacre was over.

To be fair about it, Longarm told himself, probably over half the gang had been killed or badly wounded in the explosions. That, in its way, was as cold-blooded as anything the cavalrymen had done. Longarm had never been a man to waste a lot of time on regrets. Those outlaws had slaughtered innocents in the past, and now they had reaped the whirlwind they had sown.

He picked up his rifle, which he had placed on the ground next to the leftover dynamite, and started forward. "Come on," he said over his shoulder to Morgan. "I want to check on those prisoners."

As he approached the cabin where Harriet and Uncle Dan were being held, he saw the guard sprawled on the ground, a black pool of blood spreading under his head. He must have been killed in the first volley. Longarm knelt, grimacing as he felt around in the dead man's pockets. He found a set of keys and straightened. As he began to try the keys in the padlock on the door, he called, "Harriet! Uncle Dan! It's me, Custis Long! The fight's over!"

"Custis!" Harriet cried from inside the cabin. "Oh, thank God!"

The second key Longarm tried opened the lock. He pulled it from the hasp and swung the door open. Harriet rushed out into his arms. Uncle Dan limped out after her.

"Sounded like all hell was breakin' loose out here," the old-timer said. "What in blazes happened?"

"Lieutenant Morgan and I blew up the other cabins with some dynamite we found," Longarm explained.

His arms were around Harriet, so he felt her stiffen as he mentioned Morgan's name. That didn't come as any surprise to him. She had pressed her face to his chest, but now she lifted her head and said, "Lieutenant Morgan is here?"

"That's right, Miss Summers," Morgan said from behind Longarm.

"You two don't really sound like long-lost lovers," Longarm said quietly to Harriet.

"That's because we're not," Morgan said. The metallic ratcheting of a gun hammer being eared back came from behind Longarm. "Don't move, Marshal."

Harriet looked up at Longarm. "You've figured it out, haven't you?"

"Reckon I've figured out a lot of things," Longarm said tautly. "Mainly that everybody's been lying to me pretty much all along."

"I'm sorry, Custis. I had my orders."

"Orders?" Morgan repeated. "What the hell are you talking about? By the way, don't move, Marshal, or I'll have to put a bullet through your head."

Harriet slipped back a step, out of Longarm's embrace. She looked past him at Morgan and said coldly, "Put down that gun, Lieutenant. You're under arrest."

Morgan laughed. "I don't think so, but you've got the balls of a man for saying it, Miss Summers." The other survivors from the lost patrol came up behind the lieutenant and trained their pistols on Longarm, Harriet, and Uncle Dan.

"You better listen to her, son," the old-timer said.

"Shut up, you damned old pelican. Why should I listen to either of you?"

Uncle Dan drew himself up stiffly. "That's Colonel Old Pelican to you, you murderous little jackass. Colonel Daniel Boldin, at your service."

"You ain't really her great-uncle, are you?" Longarm asked.

"As a matter of fact . . . well, no, I'm not. We're partners, though. Work for the provost marshal's office. Harriet's a civilian, but I got all the military authority we need."

"It's too bad for you I'm not a soldier anymore," Morgan said.

172

"That's right," Uncle Dan snapped. "You're nothin' but a deserter and an owlhoot, just like Vance and all them others."

Keeping his hands well away from his Colt so that Morgan and the others wouldn't get trigger-happy, Longarm half-turned toward the renegade lieutenant. "Indulge me," he said. "You and your men have been pulling those hold-ups all over West Texas for the past year, haven't you?"

"Yes, you had it right to start with, Marshal," Morgan admitted. "It was a sweet set-up, too. No one ever suspected us. We even chased ourselves that time, riding back into a settlement in our uniforms after we'd looted it earlier in the day. There's no telling how long we could have kept it up." A bitter edge came into his voice. "If that bastard Vance hadn't gotten greedy and decided that he wanted to take over."

"He set up the ambush, just like you told me a while ago?"

Morgan nodded. "That's right. He was going to be the only survivor of the original group. But he made the mistake of leaving me and these other men alive."

"That was pretty damned careless, all right." Longarm was stalling for time, but since Morgan seemed a mite talkative, he thought it was worth the gamble. He glanced at Harriet and went on, "But you were wrong about one thing: somebody did suspect you, or else the army wouldn't have sent Miss Summers and Uncle Dan to Fort Stockton to investigate."

Morgan swung the barrel of his revolver toward Harriet and said, "That's right. What about that, Miss Summers? Where did we slip up?"

She hesitated for a moment and then said, "It wasn't you, Morgan. It was Ordway."

"That son of a bitch!" Morgan exclaimed.

"He spent a little too much and let a few things slip," Harriet went on. "Just enough to make Colonel Bascomb suspicious."

"I knew it had to be either Bascomb or Ordway who kept sending those hired guns after me," Longarm muttered. "They were the only ones who knew I was going to look for that missing patrol. Ordway didn't want you boys found, of course, for fear the trail would lead right back to him. I was leaning toward him being the culprit, because he tried to talk Bascomb out of telling me about the patrol in the first place."

"Yes, yes, you're smart," Morgan snapped. "So smart you believed me and helped me wipe out Vance's bunch."

Longarm shook his head. "I wouldn't say I believed you. The more you opened your mouth, the more I knew you were lying. You didn't just find horses and guns and clothes. You raided some ranch and murdered the poor folks who lived there, didn't you?"

Morgan shrugged and said callously, "We needed those things more than they did."

"You're lower'n a snake's belly," Uncle Dan said angrily. "To think that you once wore the uniform of the United States cavalry!"

"And will again," Morgan said confidently. "After you're all dead, the five of us will ride back to Fort Stockton and tell everybody how that outlaw gang attacked us and then killed you. We'll be the heroic survivors who wiped out the desperadoes."

"You're forgetting that Colonel Bascomb is already suspicious of Major Ordway," Harriet pointed out. "He'll get to the truth sooner or later."

"Then maybe it's time for the major to have a little fatal accident," Morgan said with a grin. "Without proof, Bascomb can't do a damned thing. We'll serve out the rest of our time and then go and get all the loot we've cached. It adds up to quite a fortune, you know."

Longarm sighed. "It does seem like you've got it all covered, old son." He scratched his belly through his shirt.

"You reckon it'd be all right if I had a smoke before you killed us?"

"Why not? Keep your hand away from that gun, though."

"Don't worry about that. I don't intend to die until I've had a last cheroot."

Carefully, so that Morgan would see that he wasn't trying any sort of trick, Longarm took a cheroot from his pocket and put it in his mouth.

"Don't go digging around for a match, or anything else," Morgan said. "I'll light it for you. I've still got some of those lucifers you gave me."

He switched the pistol to his left hand and struck the sulfur match with his right. As Morgan extended his arm, Longarm glanced at Harriet and Uncle Dan, making sure where they were, and then leaned forward so that he could hold the tip of the cheroot in the flame. He puffed hard to get a good light.

As he was doing that, he brought up his left hand with a stick of dynamite held tight against his wrist. He had slipped it out from under his shirt where he had stashed it earlier, thinking it might come in handy when Morgan got around to showing his true colors. The fuse was barely two inches long, because he had pinched off most of it when he was pretending to scratch his belly a moment earlier. Before Morgan had any idea what was going on, Longarm had lit the fuse. Flame hissed toward the blasting cap with blinding speed.

Longarm tossed the dynamite at the feet of the renegade troopers.

They let out startled yells of horror and tried to dive away from the explosive, knowing there wasn't time to put out the fuse. At the same instant, Longarm lunged backward, tackling Harriet and grabbing Uncle Dan and hauling both of them through the open door of the adobe cabin where they had been held prisoner. They sprawled on the floor as Morgan's gun roared twice.

Then a much louder roar shattered the night and shook the ground underneath them. Longarm covered his head with his arms and shielded Harriet with his body as debris pelted them. As the blast died away, Longarm rolled to the side and came up on one knee. His hand swept the Colt from the cross-draw rig on his left hip. He looked through the open doorway, but all he could see was a cloud of smoke and dust that made him cough as some of it rolled into the cabin. He fumbled out a match and snapped it into life on his thumbnail.

Then a ghastly apparition came out of that cloud shrieking incoherent curses of rage. The force of the blast had picked up Morgan and slammed him face-first into the adobe wall of the cabin. His nose was flattened and the other bones in his face must have been shattered because it was pushed out of shape until it barely resembled something human. Blood covered his features.

But somehow Morgan was still conscious and on his feet. He lunged at Longarm, clearly intent on revenge.

Longarm got a shot off that drove into Morgan's chest, but the renegade lieutenant's momentum carried him on. He crashed into Longarm and knocked the big lawman over backward. Morgan scrabbled at Longarm's throat, trying to lock his fingers around it in a chokehold. Longarm slammed his Colt into the side of Morgan's already misshapen skull.

Then something else hit Morgan and knocked him off of Longarm. Several thuds sounded inside the cabin, although Longarm heard them only dimly because he was still a little deafened from the dynamite blast. He had dropped the match when Morgan ran into him, but he found another one and lit it.

The flickering glare showed him Morgan's limp form lying on the ground. Harriet stood over him, what was left of a little three-legged stool clutched in her hand. From the looks of Morgan's head, she had walloped him several times with the stool, although it was hard to say since he had already suffered so much damage in the explosion.

One thing was sure: he wouldn't be getting up again. He was dead.

"Stay here," Longarm said to Harriet and Uncle Dan as he came to his feet. He dropped the match and slipped out of the cabin, the Colt held ready in his fist. Groaning led him to two of the outlaw cavalrymen, who had been seriously wounded in the blast. Another one lay nearby, having already bled to death from the leg that had been blown right off him.

That left one man unaccounted for, and he came stumbling out of the darkness toward Longarm, firing as he lurched forward. Longarm threw himself to the side as he heard the wind-rip of a slug beside his ear. He caught himself on his left hand and triggered the Colt in his right, firing twice. The bullets spun the final trooper around and dropped him in a limp heap to the ground.

It was over, Longarm thought as he pushed himself to his feet. In a bloody half-hour, in the middle of an ancient volcano under a serene moon, an entire outlaw gang and the survivors from another had been wiped out. El Solitario had seen fire and death many times before over the eons and now those silent stone walls had witnessed violence once more.

And when he and his companions were gone, once more it would stand alone, a monument of sorts, a reminder of just how puny and transitory these humans were with their petty struggles.

Chapter 20

The two wounded outlaws died before the night was over, so in the morning it was just Longarm, Harriet, and Uncle Dan who rode away from El Solitario, leading long strings of horses. They had salvaged a lot of supplies and they had also found a considerable amount of cash, although not as much as the fortune Morgan had talked about.

"I don't reckon this is all of the loot, just what Vance's bunch got from those jobs in Ozona and Marathon," Uncle Dan speculated as they rode. "El Solitario is mighty far away from Fort Stockton. I think when Morgan was runnin' the gang, they must've had a hide-out somewheres else, more convenient to the fort."

"Maybe Major Ordway can tell us where that is when we get back," Harriet said. "The rest of the money is probably there."

"I'm glad it wasn't Colonel Bascomb who was working with Morgan," Longarm commented. "He seemed like a pretty good officer. Did he know that you two were working undercover for the provost marshal?"

Harriet shook her head. "No, even though the colonel was the one who grew suspicious of Major Ordway and asked for help, we decided it would be better to keep him in the dark about who we really are, at least for the time being. And then you showed up and started off on the trail of the gang, so we decided to tag along."

"Speaking of tagging along, what happened to that mutt?" Longarm asked. "He was with you when Vance's men jumped you, wasn't he?"

"Yes, but he ran off when the shooting started. He's probably gone wild by now. I'm glad he got away rather than being shot."

Contrary to Harriet's prediction, when they got back to the wagon a couple of days later, Tag was sitting there waiting for them, his tongue lolling out and his tail wagging. He looked like he was asking them what took them so long.

Uncle Dan chortled, obviously glad to see the mutt. "Dang critter! Trust a good-for-nothin' dog to go back to where he knows he'll get fed."

"He's not good for nothing," Harriet objected as she dismounted and hugged Tag's shaggy neck. "He just knew he couldn't stand up to half a dozen gun-toting outlaws. Pretty smart, if you ask me."

Tag just slobbered and grinned.

It caused quite a commotion when the wagon rolled into Fort Stockton a few days later. They had stopped at Marathon and returned the money looted from the bank and the other businesses there, but Longarm had asked specifically that no one at the fort be notified that they were on their way back. He didn't want Major Ordway to get spooked and take off for the tall and uncut before they got there.

So their return was a surprise and as one of the troopers on duty ran to notify the sergeant of the guard, Uncle Dan drove on around the parade ground toward the headquarters building. Longarm and Harriet rode beside the wagon and the extra horses, which were tied on to the back of the vehicle, trailed behind. Soldiers trotted along after them, eager to see what was going to happen.

Uncle Dan brought the wagon to a halt right in front of the headquarters building. Someone must have carried the word inside because Colonel Bascomb stepped out onto the building's porch, followed by his adjutant.

Major Jeremiah Ordway was nowhere to be seen, Long-arm noted.

"Marshal Long!" Bascomb exclaimed. "Good to see you again. I see you found our wayward teamster, as well as his niece." The colonel glared at Uncle Dan. "As glad as I am that you've returned safely, Boldin, I'm not happy about the way you disappeared."

Uncle Dan looped the team's reins around the brake lever and grinned. "Well now, Colonel, if I was really a civilian I might be a tad worried right now, but seein' as I ain't, I'd advise you not to get too danged huffy with me."

Bascomb's eyes widened. "What did you say? You can't talk to me like that!"

The old-timer chuckled and then said, "Climb down off your high horse, Bascomb. You're a good officer and there ain't no need to get your dander up. You see, I'm a colonel, too, and I been one longer, so I reckon I outrank you."

"A colonel?" Bascomb repeated in disbelief.

"That's right," Uncle Dan said with a sober nod. "Colonel Daniel Boldin, attached to the provost marshal's office. Miss Summers ain't my niece at all. She's a civilian investigator workin' for me."

"But . . . but . . ." Bascomb sputtered. "I know I asked the provost marshal's office for help with a certain matter—"

"And you got it," Longarm broke in, "you just didn't know it at the time. Where's Ordway?"

Bascomb looked around in confusion, obviously trying to sort out everything that was coming at him with dizzying speed. "Major Ordway? I . . . I don't know—"

The sudden rataplan of hoofbeats made Longarm hip around in the saddle. He bit back a curse as he spotted a blue-clad figure on horseback, galloping away from the fort's corrals. That would be Major Ordway, he knew, the man who along with Lieutenant Morgan had masterminded the scheme that had transformed cavalry troopers into riders of the owlhoot trail. The sight of Longarm returning to the fort with Harriet and Uncle Dan had told Ordway that the jig was up.

"I'll get him!" Longarm said as he heeled his horse into motion. The animal was tired from the long ride, while Ordway was probably on a fresh mount, but Longarm wasn't going to let that stop him. He had come too far, gone through too much, to let Ordway escape now.

Leaning forward over his horse's neck, Longarm rode between a couple of adobe buildings and then out into the flatland bordering the fort. The landscape was dotted with scrub brush and mesquite trees. Longarm could see the fleeing Ordway ahead of him. He urged the horse on to greater speed.

After a few minutes he realized that he wasn't going to be able to catch the major. Gritting his teeth in anger, Longarm reined his horse to a stop and dropped to the ground. He pulled the Winchester from the saddle boot and turned the horse so that he could lay the barrel of the rifle across the saddle to steady it.

"Easy, boy, easy," Longarm breathed as he squinted over the barrel and drew a bead on Ordway. He didn't like shooting a man in the back, but under the circumstances, he didn't have much choice. He would like it even less if Ordway got away.

Longarm drew a deep breath, held it, squeezed the trigger. The Winchester cracked wickedly as it recoiled against his shoulder.

A second later, he knew he had missed the renegade major. Ordway's horse leaped in the air and then collapsed in a rolling tangle of legs that kicked up a cloud of dust. Longarm's bullet had hit the horse, not the man, and he regretted that, too.

But he didn't let it stop him from springing back into the saddle and kicking his own horse into a run. He galloped toward Ordway, who sprawled motionless on the ground, either stunned or injured by the fall. Longarm had caught a glimpse of him cartwheeling through the air as he was thrown from the saddle.

When Longarm drew within forty feet of Ordway, he reined in and swung down to the ground again. He started forward on foot, keeping the rifle trained on Ordway. Longarm wondered if the major might have broken his neck when he landed.

A moment later, he knew that wasn't the case, because Ordway suddenly rolled over swiftly and flame lanced from the barrel of the revolver in his hand. For a snap shot, it was a damned good one. The slug sizzled through the air only inches from Longarm's ear as the big lawman threw himself to the side.

He knelt on one knee and brought the Winchester to his shoulder, aiming and firing in one smooth motion. The bullet slammed into Ordway's left shoulder just as the major tried to get up. The slug's impact sent Ordway rolling over on the ground again.

"Give it up, Major!" Longarm called. "Throw down your gun and elevate!"

Instead, Ordway pushed himself up on his knees and fired again. He had managed somehow to hang on to the gun and he fired two wild shots that kicked up dirt to Longarm's left before Longarm sighed and squeezed off another round from the Winchester. The bullet struck Ordway squarely in the chest and smashed him backward. He landed on the ground with his arms and legs outflung.

This time he didn't get up as Longarm approached. The lawman could see Ordway's chest rising and falling raggedly. Blood bubbled up through the hole in his chest, staining his uniform, and a faint whistling sound told Longarm that the man was lung-shot. He probably had only minutes left to live, if not seconds.

"Just so you know," Longarm said as he stood over the dying major, "Morgan and the rest of his bunch are dead. Vance double-crossed him, set up an ambush by another gang, and took over. But he didn't kill Morgan and that was a mistake. Vance and his boys are dead, too. So that just leaves you, Ordway. If that uniform you're wearing ever meant anything to you, tell me where all the loot is cached."

Ordway gave a hollow laugh that rattled in his ventilated chest. "Go to . . . hell, Long," he gasped. "You'll never . . . find it."

"And you'll never spend any of it, you son of a bitch," Longarm said.

It was too late, though. He was talking to a dead man.

Hoofbeats made him turn around and look toward the fort. He saw Harriet, Colonel Bascomb, and several troopers riding hurriedly toward him. He went to his horse and slid the Winchester back in the saddle boot, fighting the weariness that had him in its grip. He had traveled a long, hard trail the past couple of weeks, but now it was over.

Longarm was looking forward at last to a little rest.

Harriet didn't give it to him, at least not right away. As soon as they were in his room at the Pecos House, after they had explained everything at length to Colonel Bascomb and Sheriff Dewey Arquette, she started taking her clothes off and then when she was nude went to work on his duds. Longarm found that he wasn't quite as tired as he had thought and perked up enough to go along with what she wanted.

Now, she was straddling his hips and slowly pumping back and forth as she rode his shaft. He had already emptied himself into her once, but he'd stayed hard enough to remain inside her. The slick heat they shared was mighty nice, Longarm thought as he cuddled her on his broad chest.

Harriet was a little out of breath from her own climax. When she could talk again, she asked, "What are you going to do now, Custis?"

"I figured I'd lay here and hold you for a spell," he replied with a grin.

She lifted her head and smiled down at him. "I meant after that."

"Well, I'll send a wire to Denver and tell Billy Vail how everything turned out. Then, if he doesn't have anything else for me to do in this neck of the woods, I reckon I'll head back."

"So one way or another, it's off to another job for you."

"That's about the size of it," Longarm admitted. "One thing you can count on, somebody's always breaking the law somewhere." He paused for a moment and then asked, "How about you and Uncle Dan?"

"I suspect the provost marshal will have another job for us, too," she said. "Lawbreaking isn't confined to civilians, you know."

"Yeah, Ordway and Morgan and those other troopers were proof a-plenty of that," Longarm said. "It's a shame we don't know what happened to all that loot."

"Maybe it will turn up one of these days." Harriet shook her head. "I don't want to talk about it anymore. We all came too close to dying. We would have if you hadn't thought to hide one of those sticks of dynamite under your shirt."

Longarm grinned and said, "That was a mite worrisome, running around with the damned thing tucked up right against me. I was worried that I might trip and fall and set it off."

Harriet said, "We're still talking about it," and brought

her mouth down on his to make sure that it didn't happen again.

After a few minutes of sweet, passionate kisses, she said quietly, "I was wondering about something else."

"What's that?"

"What are we going to do with Tag?"

"Leave him here at the fort, I reckon," Longarm said. "I sure as blazes can't take him with me. I got no place to keep a dog in Denver."

Although the idea of the look on Henry's face if he moseyed into the office with the big mutt at his heels did make Longarm smile . . .

"Uncle Dan and I will take him, if that's all right with you," Harriet said. "We've gotten fond of him, and he seems to like us."

"That's fine with me," Longarm told her. "The way you two work undercover, I reckon having a dog around might even come in handy sometimes."

"That's what I was thinking." Harriet nuzzled Longarm's neck. "Well, I wasn't really thinking that right at the moment. I have something else on my mind."

Her hips began thrusting more emphatically as Longarm's manhood swelled inside her. He let out a mock groan.

"Woman, I got to rest sometime!"

"Sometime," Harriet said breathlessly. "But not yet."

LONGARM

Explore the exciting Old West with one of the men who made it wild!